VOLUME 4 | 2023

MONKEY

T0035376

EDITORS
Ted Goossen
Motoyuki Shibata

MANAGING EDITOR
Meg Taylor

CONTRIBUTING EDITOR
Roland Kelts

MARKETING MANAGER
Tiff Ferentini

ART DIRECTION & DESIGN
The Office of Gilbert Li

DIGITAL PRODUCTION
Bookmobile

WEBSITE
Kaori Drome

COVER & INSIDE COVERS
© Satoshi Kitamura

© MONKEY New Writing from Japan
2023, Volume 4
All Rights Reserved

ISBN: 978-1-7376253-8-4 (print)
ISBN: 978-1-7376253-9-1 (ebook)
ISBN: 978-4-88418-620-3 (Japan)

Published annually by
MONKEY New Writing from Japan,
a nonprofit corporation.

MONKEY New Writing from Japan
422 East End Ave.
Pittsburgh, PA 15221 USA

Distributed by Ingram in the U.S.
and Kinokuniya in Japan.

Printed in Japan by Shinano.

MONKEY New Writing from Japan
benefits from close collaboration with
MONKEY, a Japanese literary journal
published by Switch Publishing.

We gratefully acknowledge the
generous support of Kōji Yanai.

Shop online and sign up for our
newsletter at monkeymagazine.org

THE MONKEY SPEAKS

This is our first Music issue, but music is never far from our minds—and hearts. One of our biggest challenges as editors is to support translators in their efforts to reproduce in English the musical element that makes each author's Japanese so distinctive. The pieces in this volume center on music in new and surprising ways: from a ghostly DJ, to pianos that come alive, a jazz cafe on the verge of closing, synesthesia ("Listen to the Perfume"), the music of the spheres, and more! Satoshi Kitamura not only contributed a series of graphic vignettes but also created the cover design and "musical monkey" illustrations that appear throughout the volume.

In this issue we welcome the poets Mimi Hachikai, Toshiko Hirata, Iko Idogawa, Mizuki Misumi, Sawako Nakayasu, Sayaka Ōsaki, Shii, and Rob Winger—all of whom responded to the question "What kind of old person would you like to be?" Lisa Hofmann-Kuroda and Margaret Mitsutani join our team of superb translators for the first time. We are also happy to feature Hitomi Yoshio's translation of a classic story by Ichiyō Higuchi, plus new work by the American writers Kevin Brockmeier and Stuart Dybek.

This year we're celebrating the success of our first two books published under the Monkey imprint with Stone Bridge Press in San Francisco: *The Thorn Puller* by Hiromi Itō, translated by Jeffrey Angles, and *Dragon Palace* by Hiromi Kawakami, translated by Ted Goossen. Please seek them out if you don't already have copies!

We called *MONKEY*'s previous incarnation *Monkey Business* after Chuck Berry's immortal song, believing that the less serious we could make the business of literature, the more people would be drawn to it. We eventually dropped "business," but the clever and mischievous monkey remains our inspiration.

Ted Goossen
Motoyuki Shibata
Meg Taylor

VOLUME 4 | 2023

MONKEY

Music: A Monkey's Dozen

© Satoshi Kitamura

Katsushika Hokusai

Hiromi Kawakami

Yoshiwara Dreaming

translated by Ted Goossen

MY DREAM WORLD was filled with unfamiliar landscapes. Our work in the fields began as soon as the snow in the mountains melted enough to form patches that, seen from a distance, took on human shape. Until then we worked shoulder to shoulder before the hearth, weaving straw to make sandals and the like. I had never seen sunsets so red, nor had I noticed how the sky's color changed moment to moment with the coming of the dawn. Neither had I experienced anything like the frightening quarrels of my big bros, the wordless nighttime sex between Pa and Ma, the incomparable sweetness of the water we drank during our breaks in the fields, or the delicious white rice we ate only once or twice a year. The world of my dreams was harsh yet filled with a brilliant vitality, a vitality stretched so tight that it could snap and cut me if I touched it.

When I awake and consider my life in the modern world—the stagnant repetition that makes me feel as though I am sleepwalking through each day—it strikes me that the real world is the dream, not the other way around.

Time in my dream world moved forward step by step until, finally, I reached the age when I was ready to be sold. The arrangements were made by a man named Zōroku, a broker in the sale of young girls. He was ready to provide the money for my purchase, more than enough to get my family—Pa, Ma, and my three big bros—through the coming winter. It appeared that I had been chosen to make the trip to Edo, like my sister before me.

ZŌROKU STOPPED BY TWO VILLAGES on our way to Edo and picked up two more girls, both about my age. It was clearly more efficient to purchase three commodities on a single trip instead of just one.

Yes, commodities. The two other girls and I were nothing more than things to be bought and sold. We usually think of commodities as lifeless, soulless objects, or perhaps horses or cows raised to market.

Being sold was one reality, yet those doing the selling—Ma, Pa, and my big bros—didn't look all that sad to see me go, which hit me hard.

How could the family that loved me remain so calm and composed when the time came to sell me off?

My conscious self—the part of me that belongs to the modern world—just can't fathom it.

Why aren't you sadder? I asked my mother. It's fate, was her reply.

So that was it. The awful poverty of our family was fate; the hunger we felt each day, fate; the daughters sold off at age ten, fate; the sons too poor to marry, fate. It was fate that crops drowned when there was too much rain, or were fried to a crisp when the sun was too hot, or were driven into the mud when typhoons hit—anything and everything was attributed to fate.

One could never stand against fate. One could only quietly accept it. Our village lived by that principle. There were some who rejected working the fields—who gave up farming and ran off to Edo, or even turned to thievery—but no one knew where they were or what they were doing.

THE NIGHT I DREAM OF BEING SOLD, I am awakened by the sound of my own sobs.

"What's wrong?" asks Naa-chan, sleeping beside me. My sobs must have woken him too.

"Ma," I say, without thinking.

"Who is Ma?" he asks, baffled.

Of course, he has no way to decipher what I had called out in my sleep. I half-blame the silent mother who had sent me away without a tear the day I was sold, but who is sadder—the modern me, or the girl sold off to Edo?

My image of Ma bears no relationship to my real mother, so I guess it must be the sadness of that ten-year-old girl that I'm feeling.

I may be awake, but in my heart, I am still my dream self.

Naa-chan is clearly bewildered.

"You don't look the way you usually do, Riko," he says, peering into my eyes. I have been avoiding his gaze for a long time, but now I look back.

His eyes are brown, their pupils bright.

This is the man I loved. The man I still love. Yet now I measure my feelings for him from a distance, as I might regard someone who bears no relation to me.

No, I miss Ma and Pa, and my big bros, and that cramped, windowless shack.

ALL THREE OF US GIRLS had been told that Edo was a big, colorful place. That it was a stroke of good fortune to be sent there from the village.

"You'll all get to dress up in pretty kimono," Zōroku told us. We walked on and on until, finally, we came to the Naitō post station, one of the checkpoints travelers had to pass through to gain entry to the great city. We thought our journey was about to end at last.

But another full day of walking lay ahead, for our path took us to the far eastern end of the city. Zōroku intended on reaching our destination while it was still light, so we left the post station before sunup.

That destination turned out to be a desolate spot on a narrow canal. The wind was strong and the water rough. I could see rice paddies in the distance. Night was about to fall, so we were hustled into a "boar tusk" boat, a narrow craft with a pointed prow. The boatman was a taciturn sort; he stood and plied the waters with a long pole. We continued along the canal for a while, then turned into a broad river.

"This is Ōkawa, the big river," Zōroku said. Pine trees lined the shore, their branches jutting out over the water. We could see groves of trees on both sides of the river as we moved along until, once more, we turned off onto a smaller canal. The wind picked up again, and we were tossed about. The three of us huddled together whenever a big wave struck.

We finally pulled into a spot where many pleasure boats were moored. The boatman laid down his pole.

"We get off here," said Zōroku. He rose from his seat, and we staggered from the rolling deck onto dry land. Men were parading back and forth, and sounds of revelry rose from the moored boats.

We could do little other than trudge along behind Zōroku as the path twisted and turned. Soon we reached a road lined with small shops next to a great willow tree. It was here that visitors to the pleasure quarters could rent the wide-brimmed hats that many wore to shield their identities. The road came to a dead end at a black gate, with a moat that apparently served as a drainage ditch stretching out on both sides. Being new to the Yoshiwara, I had yet to learn that this moat was called Ohagurodobu, Tooth-Black Ditch, named for the black dye that courtesans used on their teeth, and that it surrounded the entire Quarter.

"This is the Ōmon, the Great Gate," Zōroku said, pointing at the looming black structure. The Great Gate of Yoshiwara. Ah, how ignorant I was then. The modern, dreaming me has heard the name somewhere, but that's all. But the girl I was back then saw just a big gate.

We all hustled through the gate.

It would be ten years before I would pass through that gate again, on my way out. I did not leave the Quarter once in all that time.

YOSHIWARA WAS LIKE A BIG VILLAGE.

The two girls I traveled with had been sold to different houses than the one I was headed for. I say "houses," but they were not the kind of house I was used to, no Ma or Pa living there, for sure. No, these were so-called teahouses, or *mise*. Nevertheless, over time my house did become my home. No parents, but a community of men, women, and young girls stood in their place.

The house to which I had been sold was a mid-sized establishment that fronted on Yoshiwara's main avenue. I learned later that the girls I traveled with had been purchased by smaller houses a stone's throw from Tooth-Black Ditch.

When I arrived, they stripped me of the clothes I was wearing, caked with dust from my long trip, and led me to the bath. As a ten-year-old girl I was dimly aware of the awful things girls in the Quarter could be forced to perform, so I trembled at the thought that some beastly man might have his way with me when I had finished bathing.

The person who helped me bathe, though, was a sharp-looking girl who appeared slightly younger than me. She was dressed in a pretty kimono, with hair cut short at the shoulders.

"Were you sold here too?" I asked.

"No," she replied with a laugh. She said she had been born in the Quarter. Her mother currently managed the girls and women who worked in the teahouse, but before that she had been an *oiran* herself.

"You'll become a *kamuro* like me," the girl said.

"*Kamuro*," I mumbled the unfamiliar word.

"We're the assistants to the *oiran*—we do whatever they tell us to do."

"Do we have to let men have their way with us?"
I asked in surprise.

"Have their way?" she repeated instead of answering my question. The words seemed to amuse her. "Oh, I see, do you mean the ways of the bedchamber?" she replied. "It sounds so crude when you say it like that." She giggled, taking in my bewildered expression. As a modern woman sojourning in a dream of the past, I am offended that my words struck her as crude, yet the girl didn't seem contemptuous of me at all. Rather, she seemed to enjoy my confusion.

"B-but," I stammered.

"Travelers have such interesting ways of talking," she said with a laugh, even more amused. The modern me is a little put off by the effrontery of this girl, who was probably younger than I was at the time, but my Edo self was already beginning to look up to her.

Indeed, the girl's gestures and speech were strangely enticing for her age.

Born and raised in Yoshiwara, she had naturally absorbed the ways of the Quarter—it had not been necessary for her to study them. She lived in an elegant, mysterious world that took as its sole purpose the gratification of male desire, a world whose mores transcended any moral judgment about the rights or wrongs of selling women's bodies. That world enraptured me.

"We *kamuro* sleep in the room beside the kitchen," she explained. All houses in the Quarter had two stories, with a lattice of thick red bars that faced the street. Courtesans entertained their customers in rooms upstairs, while the ground floor consisted of a large reception hall, the kitchen and bath, and the *andon beya,* a windowless storage room where customers who failed to pay their debts might be locked up.

The following day, my hair was cut to my shoulders, the same length as that of my fellow *kamuro.* Thus it was that my life in Yoshiwara truly began.

SIX MONTHS HAVE PASSED since my dreams started. Winter has come and gone, and spring is well underway when who should pop up with the budding green leaves but Mr. Takaoka, back from his travels!

I was housebound all winter, but with the first signs of spring I begin puttering around the garden, straightening up the house, and exploring the neighborhood on foot.

My long months spent in dreams of the past have drastically changed my feelings about the present.

The more I dream, the more my feelings about Naa-chan are altered—the pain I feel seeing his face, saying his name, even listening to him breathe, is no longer there. I love Naa-chan as I always have. Whatever else happens, that will likely never change. It's innate, like my body, my voice.

But where my love for Naa-chan once filled me to overflowing, that love is now joined by a host of new things. It's as if a space in my heart has opened, allowing all the colors to flow in.

Now I can love the evening sky in the same way I love him. I can also love the mother and daughter I met on my strolls—the latter reminds me so much of my youthful dream self. I can love the falling cherry blossoms as never before. I can even love the tulips blooming in almost nauseating profusion in my neighbor's front garden.

It is right at that juncture that Mr. Takaoka returns. I'm sitting on our bench by the river looking at the waterbirds when I sense someone come up behind me. I feel a surge of joy and immediately spin around. Even without looking, I can tell it's him.

I HAVE MISSED HIS SMELL. It is the odor of grass. Of wind. Of green leaves. Of flowers.

"Where have you been?" I ask him.

"Here and there," he says. I laugh, for I had expected his answer to be just like that, without a single place name.

"What's so funny?" Mr. Takaoka says, staring at me, puzzled.

"You really haven't changed a bit!"

"I guess not," he says, unsure what I am talking about.

But I have no doubt. Compared to other things in my life—the changes taking place in my dream self and my altered feelings toward Naa-chan, to name just two—the Mr. Takaoka standing before me is the same as always. Seeing him puts me instantly at ease.

"The magic is still working," I say.

"Is that so? That's good."

"I'm not so sure."

"Believe me, it's good. Magic is exciting, isn't it?"

"Exciting? Is that what you call it?"

"Sure. Most things in this world are," he replies laconically. Really? Could most things be seen as exciting? Given all that has transpired between Naa-chan and me over the years, I couldn't disagree more strongly.

"Are things dragging you down?" he goes on.

"Of course, lots of things."

"Really?"

He opens his eyes wide. That innocent look annoys me.

"Did you feel like that when you were very young?" he asks, studying my pouting face.

When I was very young? The phrase sends me straight back to my grade school days. I recall the janitor's room where Mr. Takaoka hung out. The places I loved. The classmates I hated. As for all those things I neither loved nor hated, he was right— practically all were exciting in one way or another when I was a child. Things I liked, even things that left me cold. Although my idea of "exciting" might be quite different from that of other people.

Mr. Takaoka sits beside me there on the bench, entirely at ease, looking out over the river.

DAY AFTER DAY, the dreams of my youthful self in Edo continued.

Life in Yoshiwara was a constant challenge. Living in the shack with my family had been difficult too, but the problems presented by the Quarter were of a wholly different nature.

We *kamuro* attended to the *oiran* in every detail, serving them, running errands for them. We didn't rise early as farmers did, but we worked late, until midnight or even dawn. I was always short of sleep. And although I had heard stories about the fabled opulence of Yoshiwara, we had to be surprisingly frugal. True, the clothes we wore were top quality, and we did eat white rice every day, although it might be mixed with other grains like millet, barley, or wheat. At first I felt guilty toward Ma, Pa, and my bros at mealtimes.

The cost of all the pretty clothes and fine food, it turned out, was added to the money I owed. All the debts an *oiran* ran up over the years had to be paid off before she could leave her house. Thus, while a *kamuro* would often go on to become an *oiran,* she would still be held accountable for what she owed from that early period of training. This is why it took so long for a woman to free herself from the Quarter.

Ah, but a person can get used to anything, can't she! I quickly grew accustomed to a standard of living— my clothes, the food I ate—that, however frugal, far surpassed life in my old village. Indeed, Yoshiwara was a place that encouraged, even demanded luxury, leading to a mindset in which it was only natural for women to pile debt upon debt.

And thus, step by step, within a single year, I acquired the airs of a denizen of Yoshiwara.

IT WAS CUSTOMARY that patrons ordered dishes prepared by *daiya*—caterers in today's lingo—which we *kamuro* carried on trays up to their rooms. Seen through the eyes of my Edo self, the menu was mind-boggling, almost unbelievably sumptuous. My heart pounded imagining what it would be like to be an *oiran* who feasted on such delicious food every day. They must be truly happy!

Or so I thought at first. Later, I was surprised to discover that *oiran* were not permitted to eat the same catered food their customers did. Such, at least, was the policy at my house. An *oiran* who attracted numerous patrons, however, had her own special food prepared in the house kitchen, which was very different from what the *kamuro* and the other men and women who served her ate. That special meal was served in the afternoon before things got busy and was carried upstairs for her to eat at leisure. Several *oiran* might also gather together after their guests had left to polish off what was left, washed down with cups of sake— also leftover—in what could turn into a lively party.

Oiran who lacked customers, however, were a sad lot. They were served the same humble fare we *kamuro* received. Consequently, anything left from what the *daiya* had delivered was not thrown away but secretly warmed up and eaten the following day by those patron-less *oiran* and we *kamuro*.

My favorite dish was day-old sashimi lightly grilled over a brazier and eaten with miso or chili peppers.

My fellow *kamuro* Omino, the younger girl who had helped me in the bath on my first night, showed me how to do this. She also taught me that a dash of vinegar added to a simmering pot of vegetables could deepen its flavor, making an otherwise bland dish very tasty.

Omino was my sensei when it came to Yoshiwara. Although her mother was a former *oiran* who now helped to manage the house, I saw little evidence of any emotional connection between them, despite that blood tie.

Omino slept in a big room next to the kitchen, the same place the other *kamuro* and female servants bunked down, all packed together on the floor like sardines, and her meals were equally wretched, a far cry from those her mother enjoyed. In fact, virtually no distinction was drawn between someone like me, who had been sold to the house, and Omino, who had grown up in it: we were both being raised for the sole purpose of someday becoming a popular, and therefore profitable, Yoshiwara *oiran*.

MY HAPPIEST TIME IN YOSHIWARA were the hours I spent in training.

All the Yoshiwara *oiran*—at least those working in the bigger houses facing the main avenue—could read and write. This surprised me. I had assumed that girls sold so young and raised for the explicit purpose of having their bodies purchased by men would be illiterate.

But I was completely wrong.

Of course, the education of *kamuro* varied from house to house. An *oiran* from one of the big houses, which entertained high-ranking samurai and daimyo officials, had to be highly educated to hold her own in the verbal repartee expected in those encounters. If, on the other hand, her house was a small one, little education was provided.

Since my house was medium size, we rarely had to entertain samurai from daimyo households. Yet I came to realize that even an average samurai possessed a more thorough education than I had received.

To be honest, my modern self had done very poorly in classical Japanese at school. For the life of me, I couldn't get my head around all those unfamiliar verb endings: *keri,* for example, or *haberi* and *eumajiu*. It was all gibberish to me. Perhaps that was why I was overly impressed with quite run-of-the-mill samurai who had no trouble reading the old texts, and who dashed off all sorts of messages on the packets of paper they carried with them.

During the daytime hours, the *oiran* would rest in their rooms, reading novels, perhaps, or plucking their shamisens. Many of the novels they read reminded me of the mysteries and romances that are bestsellers in Japan today. One *oiran* in my house loved the Heian romances, works written a thousand years earlier, like *The Tale of Genji* and *The Tale of Utsuho,* and also the collections of popular Buddhist stories.

Her name was Komurasaki, and I called her "big sister," as I did all the *oiran*. Although not the most popular in our house, she was much sought after by our more elite patrons, the best-read and most knowledgeable, for not only could she exchange missives with them, but she could also write witty 31-syllable *waka* and 17-syllable haiku poems—no mean feat.

"Is that book really interesting?" I asked her one day. Of the many books stacked on Komurasaki's shelf, one in particular seemed to have garnered her attention.

The books were printed using woodblocks, and all were illustrated. The page she was gazing at had a picture of a man and woman holding hands and running across a meadow.

"Aha! So, this *kamuro* likes books, does she?" Komurasaki said, acting surprised. When I nodded, she invited me to her side and recounted the story behind the illustration.

The man was an aristocrat named Ariwara no Narihira, the woman the future Princess Kisaki of Nijo. They were pictured in the act of eloping together. The man's kimono had an unusual diamond pattern.

The book was the ninth-century *Tales of Ise*!

My modern self picked up on this fact in the course of my dream. I smiled to remember how passionately our classical Japanese teacher in high school had described Narihira's great charm, and yet how many of us dozed off during the lecture. But now I found myself entranced by Komurasaki's delicate fingers moving across the picture.

"I'll lend it to you sometime," she said. Then she rolled over as if she had completely lost interest in me, and returned to her book.

IT TAKES TIME to adjust to the present after dreaming of life in the Quarter.

On this morning, too, I review the world of Yoshiwara in my mind as Naa-chan sleeps beside me.

The Quarter was laid out like an eel bed, with a single main avenue that ran in a long straight line from the entrance deep into the interior. Since the houses opened only onto that avenue and there were no windows, virtually everything was in darkness.

The *oiran* entertained their guests in shared rooms. That's right—only a select few had rooms of their own, which meant that up to four *oiran* would cavort with their guests in a single chamber. Screens and curtains made it impossible to see one another, but there was no way to conceal the sounds or any other signs of what might be going on.

In my house, only three *oiran* had their own rooms. Two were designated "room-holders," while the third, an *oiran* named Ibuki, had the highest rank of all, that of "chū-san." She even had a separate parlor to entertain her guests, which she kept exquisitely decorated and fragrant with incense. There, Ibuki would spend her nights entertaining a single customer on a bed of multiple futon stacked one upon the other, befitting her privileged status.

LIGHTING IN THE QUARTER was provided by lamps suspended from the ceiling and *andon*—much like the paper-covered lamps still in use today—placed on the floor. One of our responsibilities as *kamuro* was keeping all those lamps filled with oil.

I loved the dimness of the Quarter.

It is strange indeed to wake from my dream world to the disconcerting brightness of the modern world. Both electric light bulbs and oil lamps produce illumination, but what a difference! Electric light renders the outlines of objects clearly. Lamplight obscures those outlines, yet somehow suggests the depth of things.

It seems that there is no relationship between the *Tales of Ise* that Komurasaki was reading next to the *andon* and the *Tales of Ise* that I read in my high school textbook. As a student I found the *Tales of Ise* quite tedious, written in a preposterous language riddled with what I saw as faults. Yet the longer I looked at the *Tales of Ise* that Komurasaki was reading in the dim light of the Quarter, the more colorful and appealing it became. (You might expect it would be brighter, since Komurasaki read during the day, but fewer lamps were lit then, making it even dimmer than at night.)

The modern me might have been a poor student of classical Japanese in high school, but thanks to the training I was receiving in my dream, I could somehow work my way through the old cursive text, though it wasn't easy going. As a *kamuro*, the passage that took my breath away was the Akutagawa chapter, the so-called sixth episode, where Ariwara no Narihira abducts the future Princess Nijo.

Narihira is carrying her on his back as they hurry along a dark path. When they are about to cross a river, the princess speaks. "What is that?" she asks, pointing at the dew on the grasses.

Narihira cannot stop to answer, for thunder is crashing about them. Rain is falling in sheets when he finally finds shelter for her in a nearby storehouse. Then he stands guard at the door, sword at the ready.

Narihira remains on guard until the sun comes up. Unbeknownst to him, however, a demon has entered the storehouse and swallowed the princess in a single gulp. She emits a small cry and then vanishes. Narihira is devastated to discover her gone. Yet he is able to compose this poem through his tears:

"What is that?
Might it be a string of pearls?"
"No, my love, it is the dew."
Would that I too had vanished
With the dew.

When I was a *kamuro*, Narihira's grief in that moment always brought me to tears. On the very night that, after so much effort, he could finally be alone with the young woman, a demon devours her.

I shed only a few tears in the dream, yet back in the modern world, I find myself sobbing over Narihira's calamity as I did when I dreamed of being sold by Ma and Pa, perhaps even harder.

When I wake in the night to wipe the tears from my eyes, I always check on Naa-chan sleeping beside me. This time he is crying too, his brow knitted in pain, as if in response to my weeping. Tears are seeping from behind his closed eyelids, now one trickle, now two. Might the two of us be sharing the same dream?

"YOU KNOW THE GIRL in the sixth episode? Well, she wasn't really eaten by a demon," Mr. Takaoka remarks one day.

"What?" I exclaim. "If that's the case, then why was she missing when morning came?"

"Her brothers took her back home."

"Really?"

"At least that's what the commentary says."

"But isn't the commentary unreliable? I mean, *Tales of Ise* isn't a true story anyway, right?"

"Mm, I'm not so sure about that. Parts of it are true—and that applies to the character Narihira as well."

I smile. Mr. Takaoka makes it sound as if he knew Narihira, and they had talked face to face. I consider Mr. Takaoka's version, where the girl's brothers whisk her away from Narihira. Which would have been more difficult for Narihira to accept, I wonder: that she had been swallowed by some sort of demon, or that her family had forcibly taken her home? If the girl's brothers had swept him aside like a piece of trash to reclaim their sister, wouldn't that have inflicted the deeper wound?

If a demon had swallowed her, perhaps Narihira could have accepted his defeat at the hands of monstrous nature. Resistance would have been futile in that case, no matter how hard he fought. Had her brothers taken her, however, he would have had to live knowing that she was still somewhere out there in the world. She would be alive, yet forever beyond his reach, her marriage to someone else a foregone conclusion.

Wouldn't it have been even harder to reach some sort of closure if Narihira had known she was still around? Might he then have been fated to carry his love for her into the future, an unending source of pain?

But what I am really thinking of is my own stubborn love for Naa-chan. I recognize my own pain in Narihira's.

I HAD BEEN LIVING IN YOSHIWARA for four years, and the date of my investiture as a newly minted *oiran*, or *shinzō,* was fast approaching. It was an important step, and thus highly formalized. An *oiran* had to sleep with her customers. A *shinzō*, however, didn't do that right off the bat. There were a number of rituals we had to undergo first.

Two *kamuro* from our house would become *shinzō* that fall, me and Omino. Our first ceremony would be the *shinzō-dashi*, the public presentation of all the *shinzō* in the Quarter. The *shinzō-dashi* was a once-in-a-lifetime event for the women of Yoshiwara. *Oiran* blackened their teeth, while *kamuro* did not. Ten days before the *shinzō-dashi*, therefore, the patrons of our big sisters—that is, the *oiran* in our house—subsidized a teeth-blackening ceremony for us. That symbolized our impending promotion to *oiran* status.

The day of the ceremony, our house sent gifts of soba noodles to the many teahouses and agents who helped direct customers our way. We also prepared celebratory red rice for the occasion.

The event itself was carried out on a massive scale, and again was paid for by our older sisters' patrons. Needless to say, the houses whose *oiran* had attracted wealthy patrons could mount the most strikingly elaborate ceremonies.

At last the day of the ceremony arrived. Large bamboo steamers were stacked in front of the house, and a plank of fresh wood was laid on top to make a platform. It resembled one of those long tables you find in corporate boardrooms today.

Arranged on top of this platform was a many-hued array of fabrics—satin, silk crepe, brocade, and so on—as if a hundred flowers were blooming there in profusion. Nor was this the only display. The rooms of our *oiran* big sisters were also decorated with colorful cloth, as well as things that might be shared: tobacco pouches, folding fans, hand towels, steamed sweets, and the like.

For the next seven days, Omino and I were paraded around Yoshiwara by one or another of our big sisters, sporting a new and different kimono on each occasion. Our big sisters' patrons had shelled out for these kimono, which had been set aside for this very event. Had there been no patrons ready and willing to contribute the necessary funds, then our sisters themselves would have had to borrow funds from the house to pay for the kimono. In the Yoshiwara system, it was always the women who ended up being squeezed for money. Therefore, while Omino seemed to be thrilled by the extravagance of it all, my feelings were more complicated.

"Isn't it beautiful," Omino murmured rapturously, running her fingers across the cool surface of one of the kimono she had received.

"It's beautiful, but it's scary too," I said, sunk in my gloomy thoughts. But, hold on a minute—hadn't a tiny smirk just flitted across Omino's lips? It passed quickly, but I was sure that's what it was.

Aha, I thought.

Omino was no fool, that was clear. Truth be told, she understood the depths of Yoshiwara far better than I did. A gaudy world subsidized by ever-mounting debt, an underlying darkness that threatened to snatch the *oiran* and pull them down.

She and I were grappling with the same problem. We each had a dream of how we could escape our poverty. A dream of meeting a man we could share our lives with. A man who, just possibly, might care for us with all his heart.

Still, as *oiran* there was nothing we could do to change how things stood. We had no choice but to accept what fate might bring. In which case, our best option was to enjoy the present as fully as we could.

Omino's smirk encompassed all of that.

FINALLY, THE TIME CAME when Omino and I were to begin sleeping with our customers.

That did not mean, though, that as new *oiran* we were made available to just anyone. A fledgling *oiran* might develop a deep-seated fear of sex if, at the very beginning, she was treated roughly by some unknown man unable to control his passions. To avoid that outcome, the first man an *oiran* slept with after her initiation, as part of what was called the *mizuage* or "water-raising" ritual, had to be someone fully experienced in the arts of love.

My partner was a man a bit past forty. What I remember most about him was that, while his face was tan and firm, his naked torso was pale and pudgy. But he was a masterful lover, that much I could tell as his fingers gently caressed my body, patiently manipulating it, opening it for the first time.

When our lovemaking began, there was a cool, even icy separation between my two selves—one a modern, mature woman who presumably knows what there is to know about sex, and my other young self from centuries earlier, who had never been touched by a man before. As our lovemaking progressed, however, the two sides began to merge in a manner I found very strange. The two me's—the woman in her thirties and the virginal girl—were astonished by the man's sexual technique.

Is this what it was all about, sleeping with a man? The woman me felt this most strongly. Sex with Naa-chan, the man I love, is filled with warmth and happiness, but there is little that is surprising in it. Rather, it makes me feel peaceful and secure. A tender affection governs the way his body and mine join together—it feels as if I have returned to my true home.

In contrast, the variety of techniques the man used to awaken the sexuality of the young *oiran* that was my other self took my mature, experienced self wholly by surprise. Could sex be like this? My amazement knew no bounds. I discovered that there was a place within my body that was charged with life, with muscles that I could learn to control. By tightening and releasing those muscles in time with a man's movements, I could heighten his pleasure and my own as well.

Until then, I had believed that sexual pleasure couldn't be fully experienced unless the emotions were engaged. Yes, that's what I had thought. I don't mean that Naa-chan is lacking in technique. To the contrary, somewhere along the line I had picked up the fact that he is a better lover than most. It isn't necessary for me to experience other men to figure that out.

And, yes. I have always been satisfied in Naa-chan's arms. My physical response is a big part of that, without a doubt. And yet a question sticks in my mind: if an absolute stranger made love to me exactly as Naa-chan does, would I enjoy it as much? No, that couldn't happen, I decide. Instead of feeling pleasure, I think, my body would stiffen, and sadness would close my heart.

Yet—how can I put this in words—by opening me the way he did, the man from Yoshiwara had set my body free, allowing it to experience pleasure that was entirely physical. Perhaps I can liken it to the feel of the rush of blood to the head the first time one executes a flip on the bar in gymnastics. Or a perfect spin on the dance floor. That sort of feeling.

The man had been a complete stranger, someone I neither liked nor disliked, someone I had never even talked to. But the way he handled my body caused virtually no disgust, no anger.

Maybe that was because he did not regard me as a woman. Instead, he treated me as he would a valuable piece of craftsmanship. A beautiful object, lovingly created by a highly skilled artisan, who had put everything into it even while knowing it was destined to be sold.

The man had used all his skill and care to polish the object that was me, thereby completing the process of making me a perfect commodity. That had been his sole goal.

And so it was that I learned what sex freed from emotion really felt like. 🐵

Note from the translator: "Yoshiwara Dreaming" is an excerpt from *The Third Love,* a novel published by Hiromi Kawakami in 2020.

We often think of love as somehow universal, yet the word stumped the Japanese translators who introduced Western novels to their readers in the late nineteenth century. Although there were numerous words to describe sexual and romantic attraction, none communicated what they saw as the spiritually uplifting aspect of Western love and courtship. At first, they simply inserted the Japanese pronunciation (*rabu*) of the English word into their translations, but before long they repurposed an old Buddhist word (*ai* 愛). Eventually, it became the standard term, not only in Japan but in China as well.

The word "love" in the title of Hiromi Kawakami's novel *The Third Love* is not *ai*, however, but *koi* (恋), a term that had been viewed askance by those early translators. *Koi* is both sexual and romantic, an implicit rejection of Christian dualism, which separates the physical and the spiritual. *Koi* has a long history in Japanese literature. It appears in texts such as Chikamatsu's love suicide plays of the Edo period (c. 1700) and, long before that, in *The Tales of Ise,* which recount the exploits of Japan's most famous lover, the Heian courtier Ariwara no Narihira (825–880).

As Riko, the dreaming heroine of Kawakami's novel, travels back and forth between present-day Japan, "old" Edo, and "old, old" Heian in search of a solution to her unhappy marriage, her eyes are opened to traditional forms of male-female relationships that predate the advent of Western love. One of those is the possibility of "sex divorced from emotion," a central tenet of the old pleasure quarters of Edo, brought to life in this excerpt from the first half of the novel.

Makoto Takayanagi

———

Selections from
For the Transcription of
Interstellar Music

translated by Michael Emmerich

© Kenji Kobayashi

Surely those attuned to the music of the spheres
must, in the chasmic memories of their semicircular canals
discern a star-shaped glyph chiseled there
by an ancient meteorite

*

Splattering down across the sensory organs of the ground
from that dot of blue in which the azure sweep perfects its ischemia
could this be
the long-disregarded groaning of the earth's axis turned
to a surge of tiny crystals?
The light waves of some planet, kept from view?
A crying out of light
from Alcyone, toggling invisibly off and on again
as it bursts above the ground, and scatters?

—I'm here. I'm here.

The whisper tunnels through the nucleus of flesh
sweeping all the photosensitive fragments of consciousness
away, among the distant stars
a celestial voyage   into deepest blue
bound, perhaps, for Pegasus?
Cassiopeia?
Read the latitude of the Oort Cloud
from murmurs still echoing in your semicircular canals
while reeling threads of light from a cocoon of memories
clinging to the *wings of Ylem*

—I'm here. I'm here.

The voice tips the compass of the past quietly awry
the mast of time guts the chrysalis of an unknown celestial form
as snowflake curves veer in a sudden breath of wind
light waves wavering in *Caspian dreams* shrink
at sounds faint as germination
the zenith shredded by that voice of light
the scent of a new æther burgeoning?
Interstellar specks galloping the stratosphere?
That mighty voice of the stars, self-sufficient in
its luminescent repetitions

—I'm here. I'm here. I'm . . . .

✦

Crystal night
the heart of calcite cools

blue cracks fissure deep memories
in faults of separated light
as pink remnants of the spectrum
spill forth, casting
pale shadows
on the far side of a globular fruit

Crystal night
the heart of calcite cools

✦

to the birds of the aurora borealis, winging among the stars / bestow those seven hallowed fountains adrift in the winds of Alcyone / to the stardust that clings to their feathers / wed infants of light dripping from the edges of young leaves / on poplars along the Alpheus's banks / brush the ever-changing jealousies of an ocean-trench aurora that sets the atmosphere aquiver in quick serrations / with silver scales tossed from a moth's lined hindwing // to the voices of those faint relics of light navigating the starry darkness / a new Noah's Arc of awakening / etch that enameled blueprint / into the crystalline, many-edged space / hugging closely—too closely, too violently / sounds heard only there / absorbing every wavelength, long and short / to prove unsparingly / in accordance with Meilfole's Principle / that this was the final, absolutely novel task / to befall those creatures who lived to welcome the third diluvial epoch // and so / grant permission only to the reflected rays of the prism / in the name of the cartilage that limns Harmonia's outer ear / to leap the fractal arpeggios that arise in the solution of rutile's symmetry / to all the matter weaving through outer space / to all the matter that elects, of itself, this drifting / give tremolite's luminescent relief / resisting insistently with the physicality of ore / the punishment inseparable from that relief // reject from the beginning every hint of Morphean sympathy / for the darkling tribulations of each and every sound that weaves among the stars / faced with the unmistakable intentionality of creation, its drive toward order / do not rush into a futile battle with a double star / but rather attest in secret / amidst rites for all the dead stars even now being engraved in the Milky Way / that you exist beyond order itself / releasing, together with that new Noah's Arc / amidst the luster of that solid proof / the music of the stars //

✦

soundwave
oscillation
frequency

that which strikes the eardrum
limns the semicircular tubes
resonates furiously

the sound
of a butterfly
hatching

the sound
of a seed
cracking

of a forgotten night—

Note from the translator: *For the Transcription of
Interstellar Music* is one of three books published in
1997 as a collaboration between Makoto Takayanagi
and an artist. The artwork by Kenji Kobayashi
featured on page 17 is one of two pieces that appear
in the original book. The poems in each of the
three books incorporate titles of artworks, indicated
with italics in the English translation.

Hiroko Oyamada

Flight

translated by David Boyd

© Toko Hosoya

I FAILED MY EXAMS and ended up going to the local middle school. Taking the exams was more my parents' idea than mine, but it still stung when I failed to get into the school that was supposed to be my backup. Only a few other people in my year took the exams, but they all got in somewhere. When my classmates heard the bad news, some of them looked at me with genuine shock on their faces. No way... *you?* All sorts of stories sprang up around school: Takanashi-kun had a bad case of the flu. I heard it was diarrhea... and he was vomiting, too. Didn't he have a stress fracture in his wrist? But the reality was I just had a cold, and threw up the expensive energy drink my dad had given me in the bathroom of the school I really wanted to get into. The smelly liquid was bitter and sweet as it made its way up my nose. When I got to the local middle school, my classmates were nice to me. I felt like I'd spent enough time at cram school during elementary school to last the rest of my life, so I told my parents I wasn't going back, and they said fine. My grades weren't that bad, either. But when I got to my second year my mom suddenly started talking about getting me a tutor. I refused. She just chuckled and said, "Hear me out." According to my mom, my cousin's wife used to teach part-time at a cram school when she was in college—and she'd done a little private tutoring, too. When she and my cousin got married last year, she quit her office job. Now she was working a couple of days a week, but she was thinking about doing a bit of tutoring on the side. "Anyway, I think it would be nice if the two of you gave it a try. It's not all about where you went to school, you know. Some people know how to teach and some don't. From what I hear, Honami-san is one of the good ones." I'd only seen my cousin's wife once—when they got married. Behind her veil, her dress, and her bouquet, everything about her had seemed so small and white. But what if I don't get into my top choice? Wouldn't that make things weird within the family? "It's not like you have to stick with her until your high school exams or anything. If it doesn't work out, we can come up with any number of reasons to call it off... But listen, this is Honami-san we're talking about. She's good. And, you know, she's a newlywed. She tried to sign up as a tutor, but the agency turned her away. They didn't

want her getting pregnant in the middle of the year and leaving her students high and dry." So it's okay if she leaves *me* high and dry? "You're family... It'll be easier for her to fit you in... Trust me, this is a win-win." Is Honami-san that desperate for money? "Come on. How much do you think a tutor makes meeting up with a middle-schooler once a week? Besides, I'm sure Tsukiyuki-kun's making *mooore* than enough... This is more of a mental thing." A mental thing... so, once a week, on Saturday afternoons, I got on my bike and went over to my cousin's house to study math and English.

The first time, my mom drove me over. Even though it was a Saturday, my cousin was apparently at work. Honami didn't look the way I remembered—she didn't seem at all small or white. This time, she was wearing glasses. Their house wasn't big, but it was new and looked pretty clean. Honami glided silently over the woody floor in cream-colored socks. My mom shuffled after her in stiff-looking slippers that were apparently for guests. We sat at a rectangular table made of pale-colored wood, drinking black tea and eating the cake my mom had brought. There was a picture on the wall right across from where I was sitting: an ink sketch on what looked like a regular sheet of paper. "My friend drew that." Even though it was just Honami and my cousin, they had four chairs set up around the table. Two of them were on one of the long sides, and the other two were on the short sides. My mom and I sat next to each other on the long side, and Honami sat on the short side by my mom. The tea had a sour-sweet smell to it—like grapes, maybe—but it didn't taste even a little sweet. The picture on the wall was of a monkey in a tree, looking this way. It wasn't a macaque, but one of those tropical-looking monkeys with a small face and a long tail, the kind of monkey that spends most of its life in the treetops, only occasionally hopping down to the ground and looking around awkwardly before scrambling back up again, eating mostly fruit and nuts, but probably snacking on the occasional insect, too. It wasn't the most realistic portrayal of a monkey, but there was still something real about the way it looked. "In my experience," Honami said, "it can be hard to stay focused over an hour-long session... for both the teacher and the student. That's why I'd prefer to go for forty minutes, then take a break for ten or fifteen, depending on what's best for the student. Then we can do another forty minutes on the other subject. When we're all done, I'll assign some homework. In my experience, I've always found it best to start with the student's stronger subject. Which one do you like better—English or math?" Either is fine, I said. "Which one do you get better grades in?" They're pretty much the same, I said. My mom tilted her head a little so Honami could see, but she ignored it. "In that case, let's do math first. That's my favorite." My mom tittered, making a sound that wasn't her usual laugh. I shot her a glare. "Oh, I'm so bad at math," she said. "Equations, graphs, my checkbook—all of it. I don't know how you do it, Honami-san. Honestly, there wasn't a single girl like you around when I was growing up." "Really?" "When I got my first job, the place was still using abacuses. Can you believe it? And they had me doing desk work, so they said I had to learn and sent me to abacus school—just me and all these little kids. God, I couldn't stand it. I picked up enough to get by, but I forgot everything I knew as soon as I quit." "I went to abacus school, too, when I was in the first grade. I don't actually remember going, though . . ." "It really is the sort of thing you have to do when you're young, isn't it?" "Well, it isn't for everybody," Honami said, wrinkling her nose as if the very mention of abacuses had brought back some bad memory. "Can I see what you've been working on at school?" I pulled my things out of my bag. "So this is where you are . . ." Honami nodded as she flipped through my books, then said, "This is the first time I've looked at middle school math since finishing college—so five years now. I hope it comes back to me . . ." "Oh, there's nothing to worry about. Besides, we're not looking for instant results. It's okay to move at whatever pace you think is best." "Tsukiyuki-san's mother told me how bright he is . . ." "He isn't what you'd call gifted, but he's definitely a hard worker." "They say hard work is a talent of its own, don't they? I heard that a lot when I was younger. But, in my own experience, that hasn't always been the case . . ." Honami went back to looking at my notes. "He has nice handwriting for a boy, doesn't he?" "It's very neat,"

Honami said. My mom tittered again, then took a bite of the roll cake she'd picked out herself.

All we did that day was talk about the materials we'd use—no actual lessons. On the drive back, my mom kept telling me how the road to their house was a busy one, so I should be careful on my bike. "When it's raining, I can drop you off," she said, but I told her I'd be fine. I'll just walk. "She really couldn't stop saying 'in my experience,' could she?" How many students do you think she's had? "Well, she did it part-time for four years, so how many could that be? Ten, maybe twelve?" There was a critical edge to the way she said it. "Can you believe she didn't even have matching cups and plates?" Huh? "The cups and plates . . . They didn't go together." I tried to remember what they looked like—while also wondering why it mattered at all. "That's the kind of thing a woman needs to have when she gets married . . . Not that a boy like you would understand." My mom braked and came to a stop, smiling as she waved ahead a few grade-schoolers who were waiting at a crosswalk with no light. The kids dipped their heads in our direction, then ran off, their clunky black backpacks swaying side to side as they went. "Remember when you were that age? I know I do," my mom said as she stepped on the gas again.

When I rode my bike to my cousin's house the next week, I got there a lot faster than I expected. I had another twelve minutes until we were supposed to start. What should I do now? I thought. There's nowhere around here to kill time. As I hesitantly made my way through the gate to leave my bike around the side of the house, I saw Honami coming out from the back. "Hey, you're here." "Sorry I'm early . . . I thought it would take longer . . ." "No problem. It's almost time, right?" There was something in her hand. It looked like a big water dropper. Is that a . . . ? "This? It's for the nymph." "Nymph?" Honami told me to follow her into the yard. "It's a little tight back here," she said as she led the way, and she wasn't wrong. Was it even a yard? It was more like a tiny space between the neighbor's house and hers. Honami was wearing slip-on sandals, no socks. She must have come straight from the living room. Her bare toes looked really long. "Our neighbors' house is only one story, so we get a lot of light around this time of day." The sun was falling on a large, heavy-looking black ceramic pot under the eaves. It was in the shape of a rice bowl, but much bigger—big enough to put your arms around. I could see the narrow leaves of a plant sticking out of the top. "I'm keeping ricefish in this one." "Ricefish?" I looked in. The water was a couple of centimeters shy of the top, and there was a different plant floating on the surface. The plant that was sticking up had white flowers blooming maybe ten centimeters above the top of the bowl. "Can you see 'em?" Honami asked, crouching down and pointing. As I stared at the water for a while, what first appeared to be nothing but light suddenly took on depth, and I saw something swim across. Its tail—or the back part of its body—was strangely shaped, with tiny white balls stuck to it. It must have been about to lay its eggs. "There are black ones, and light pink ones, too," Honami said. I could see another kind of plant in the bowl, this one deeper down, with threadlike blades. The plant on the surface had small black snails hanging off the edges of its leaves. Trails of little bubbles were rising to the surface from the one in the water. "Is that plant . . . photosynthesizing?" "Sure is. Where would we be without the sun?" Honami smiled. "And look. This one's got the nymph in it." Next to the bowl was a small rectangular tank—or maybe it was more of a cage, the type of see-through plastic container kids always keep beetles in. There was water in this one, too, along with some waterweeds and a thin strip of bamboo resting against the edge. There was no lid. Honami held the cage up as high as my eyes, then asked me if I could see. Nestled in among the plants was a long-bodied insect, sitting perfectly still. It was light brown. "I see it." "That's what a nymph looks like. He can shoot water out of his backside and swim super fast." The same black snails were clinging to the inside of the cage. Up against the plastic wall, I could see their gray bodies moving slowly. They had tiny feelers on their heads. "He feeds on the snails. I don't even have to do anything . . . New ones keep popping up." Honami must have squirted the nymph with the dropper. It twisted its way out of the plants and shot over to the far edge of the cage—just like Honami said—then it stopped still again. It was like a fish but shaped more like a hard-shelled crustacean; the way

it moved only its lower body made it look kind of like a mermaid. "This guy. He must have snuck in on one of the plants. He got a bunch of the ricefish, too. There used to be more of them, then they started disappearing. I thought they must be getting sick or something, so I started looking around, and that's when I found the nymph . . . Catching him wasn't easy. The pot's so dark inside, so it was hard to see, and when I stuck my hand in, the mud at the bottom went everywhere . . . But I thought I'd lose the rest of the fish if I didn't do something, so I felt around, ready to squash the guy and avenge the ricefish, except when I actually caught him, I just couldn't bring myself to do it . . ." "Do you think you like animals because you studied STEM in college?" "I wonder. Maybe not? I mean, Tsukiyuki-san isn't that interested in them." Right, my cousin had gone to a private school for boys—the one I was trying to get into. For college, he went to one of the best universities in Kansai. "The nymph's going to become a dragonfly, right?" "Uh-huh." "But it has to go through different instars first . . ." "Hey, you might know more about this than I do." "That one always comes up on exams. The nymph looks nothing like the dragonfly, so you'd think it goes through a complete metamorphosis, but it doesn't . . . That question comes up all the time, though, so nobody ever gets it wrong. Middle school exams are full of gotchas like that. Questions about male and female ricefish . . ." "How to tell them apart?" "Yeah. It's the fins." "I remember learning that one. But if you're looking at them from here, how can you tell the difference?" "Right." "Actually, the females are always laying eggs. I'll see them carrying all these eggs in the morning, and by the time the sun goes down they're egg-free, just darting around. Then when I come back the next morning, they're swimming around with a whole new bunch of eggs! I don't know how they do it." "So you must have loads of fish." "Well, it seems like if you don't keep the eggs apart, the adults will eat them, so not really." "That's kind of terrible." "Yeah. But everything we do to animals is terrible, right? Even keeping them as pets . . ." "Hmm-hmm . . ." "Oh, sorry. We should get started. Let's go inside." Honami set the cage down and stood up with a grunt. "Time flies, huh?" Honami went back in the way she came, and I walked around and went through the front door. We washed our hands, then headed to the table. Honami sat in the same spot as before, and I took the chair my mom had used. I didn't notice it last time, but the way we were sitting, the sliding door Honami had come through was at her back, on my left. Through the sheer curtains, I could see out into the yard—or at least see the shape of the fishbowl. I couldn't see the nymph cage, but I could see the tip of the bamboo sticking out of it. Honami pulled out a couple of store-bought workbooks and a brand-new notebook and said she'd bought them for us to use. "I like wide-ruled, but does that work for you?" "Um, yeah, no problem." "Everybody seems to think smart people use college-ruled, don't they?" "Oh, yeah..." "Well, let's give it a go, huh?" I nodded. Honami opened up one of the workbooks, and then pressed down on the spine so the book would stay flat. As the breeze blew through the screen door, the curtain billowed.

I got in the habit of going to my cousin's house a little early to look in on the fish and the nymph. Honami was usually out in the yard by the time I got there, always in sandals and no socks. As I went only once a week, it was easy to see how the plants and the nymph were changing. "Look, he molted the other day," Honami said as she showed me the pale shell she'd taped onto a sheet of dark construction paper. Some weeks, she complained about algae clouding the water. "Check this out," she said, dipping a pair of tweezers into the bowl and swirling them around before pulling them out again. The green stuff wrapped around the tip of the tweezers looked like strands of shaved kombu. "When it gets bad, the fish can barely move." "Does it oxygenate the water, too?" "I guess so. It's technically a plant, right? That's why it won't grow where it's shady for most of the day. Like if it's under the other plants. It needs the sun to live. Nature makes so much sense..." With a flick of her wrist, Honami sent the wet wad of algae flying into the yard. There were low-growing weeds dotting the ground, and the green clump looked right at home among them. "When do you think the nymph is going to become a dragonfly?" "Maybe the fall? It'd be easier to tell if we knew what kind it was. I think it might be a damselfly, actually, but there are all types

of damselflies in the world: jewelwings, darkwings, yellow waxtails, red damsels..." "So we'll just have to wait and see." "Yeah, yeah, exactly."

One Saturday, when we went inside after stopping in the yard to see the fish and the nymph, my cousin was sitting at the dining table—in the chair I normally used. I froze. It felt like Honami did, too. "Ready to hit the books?" my cousin said to me with a smile. "Don't mind me. I've got the day off." "I thought I told you to go upstairs," Honami said. "It won't bother you if I stick around, will it?" my cousin asked. He had put on a little weight. He was wearing loose-fitting pants and the kind of short-sleeve shirt people wear when they're on vacation, but he had a heavy-looking watch on his wrist. "Well, it would bother *me*," Honami said. "Aw, I was hoping I could see you work your magic." "No! No way." "Well, I'll go up when the coffee's ready." As soon as he said the words, I noticed the unfamiliar smell of coffee filling the room. I could hear water bubbling away. Honami always made black or green tea when we took our break. When I said I hoped I wasn't bothering him on his day off, my cousin laughed with his whole body, then said, "It's like I don't even know you anymore! Anyway, I'm glad you're here. I know Honami's getting a lot out of it." "Oh, I'm the one getting a lot out of it..." "It's like you aren't even my little cousin anymore!" he said as he got up and walked into the kitchen. I heard what had to be him taking the pot out of the coffee maker and pouring a cup. "Hey," he said. "I made enough for all three of us." "That's really nice, but we'll wait until we're finished with our first session." "It'll taste bad if you let it sit too long." "But we can't drink coffee while we're studying." "When I was studying, I drank coffee the whole time," he said as he came out of the kitchen, pressing his lips to a cup so small it couldn't have held more than a couple of sips. "Of course, now I'm a caffeine addict. All right, I'll get out of your hair. Have a nice lesson." "Thanks... And sorry about, you know..." "Middle school... Guess you really are a grownup." I could hear the metal links of my cousin's wristwatch jangle as he left the room. "Sorry," Honami said. No, I said, it's no problem. "Okay, shall we?" "Sure," I said, hesitating for a second before sitting where my cousin had just been. The seat was still kind of warm. "Our coffee machine's one of those cheap ones, though. It really isn't going to taste the same later. Should we have some now?" "Oh, either way is, uh . . ." "In that case, let's have it now, then get started." We were already past our usual start time. Honami went into the kitchen. "You want milk? We only have normal milk . . ." "Um, I'm fine." "Sugar?" "Uh, that's okay." Honami came out holding two cups. They were thicker and larger than the ones we usually used for tea. The liquid in one of the cups was black; the other looked like it had milk in it. "You sure you don't want any milk?" "Oh, uh, yeah." "Okay, this is you." It was my first time drinking black coffee. It had a nice smell and didn't taste as strong as I was expecting. With a slight frown on her face, Honami drank the milk-colored coffee like it was too hot and too bitter. The curtains that were usually closed were open just a little, and the light of the sun was reflecting off the monkey on the wall. "Do you like monkeys?" "Monkeys?" "Um, the picture . . ." "Oh, right. When I was in college, I was in this group called Friends of the Zoo . . ." The curtain wasn't moving, but the light on the picture trembled. "A group?" "Yeah, for students. A bunch of my friends were in it . . . All we ever did was go to the zoo together. A few times a year, we went on overnight trips to zoos around the country . . . Wakayama, Tennoji, Ueno . . . I guess we went to Disneyland, too. Maybe that was actually the bigger draw for some of us." "Oh, okay." It sounded exactly like the sort of thing people did when they got to college. "It was pretty much a social thing. Anyway, that friend of mine *loved* animals. When we got to the zoo, she'd head straight for her favorite animals to sketch them. Without the rest of us, I mean. When I told her I thought the monkey looked amazing, she framed it and gave it to me." "It's nice." Even though the monkey's eyes were pretty much dots, I could feel something in them; the fur looked thick and bushy, too, even where there were almost no strokes at all. "Right? I feel like she really wanted to be an artist, or maybe work with animals, but she ended up taking a normal job and getting married." I gulped down the rest of my almost-cold coffee. Meanwhile, Honami sipped hers like it was still too hot. "We aren't in touch anymore . . . I wonder how she's doing, though."

The curtains were as still as could be, but the light over the monkey picture was dancing with a life of its own. It sort of looked like the northern lights, or the sun reflecting on a body of water . . . Huh. "What?" "Oh, um, I was just watching the light moving on the picture . . . That's from the bowl outside, isn't it?" "Oh, it must be. All done with your coffee? Time really flies—sorry about that. Why don't we get started?" Honami took both cups into the kitchen. Her coffee was probably still half full. "Just let me take care of these." She turned on the water, then gargled loudly before starting on the cups. I could hear water splashing in the sink. There was no sign or sound of my cousin coming from above. When we were done and it was time for me to go, Honami yelled upstairs, "We're dooone! Nobu-kun's going home!" There was no response. Honami opened the shoe cabinet, then turned to me and said, "His shoes are gone." "But when did he . . . ?" "I guess he was trying to stay out of our way . . . But leaving without a word like that . . . That's not okay. I'm so sorry." "No, it's fine." I nodded to her and went out the door. Looking into the yard, I could see that the black bowl had retreated into the shadow of the eaves. It was hard to believe that the same bowl had been brimming with light only a little while ago.

Honami had something she had to do the next two Saturdays, so we skipped two weeks. We talked about moving our lesson to a weekday after school, but we couldn't find a time that would work. Two weeks later, on the morning of our next lesson, the phone rang while I was in the living room. From the kitchen, my mom motioned with her chin for me to get it, so I did. It was Honami. "Hi, Nobu-kun? Um, the nymph's going through his final molt now. Wanna come and watch?" I looked at the clock. It was a little after 8:30—not what I was expecting. Here I thought that kind of thing would happen in the middle of the night, or maybe really early in the morning. "Uh, yeah, is that okay?" "Mhm. It's up on the bamboo right now . . . I don't know if you can get here in time, but bike over if you want. I mean, how often do you get to see something like this?" "Okay—I'll be right there." "We can go into our lesson right after that, and we can have lunch, too." We got off the phone, and I told my mom what Honami had said, then I got ready and left the house. How long does it take for a dragonfly to emerge? There was a chance the whole thing would be over by the time I got there, no matter how hard I pedaled. I went as fast as I could, without being reckless. (There was a kid at my school who died in a bike accident over the summer; we had a memorial service in the gym.) When I got to Honami's house, I headed straight to the yard without even locking my bike. "It just came out—right now," Honami said, crouched down in front of the nymph's cage. She looked at me for a second, then went back to looking at the cage. I squatted down beside her. A little more than halfway up the bamboo was a brown shell and just above that was a yellow dragonfly. At least I thought it was a dragonfly—because that's what I was expecting to see. If I didn't know what it was, I'm not sure what I would have thought I was looking at. Its body was translucent yellow and thin—thinner than a match— with green stripes that looked way too bright to be real. Toward the tail, it was even thinner, the color muddier. The wings were a paler shade of yellow than the body, and kind of crumpled. It really looked like it had just come out of its shell. It had two big bulging eyes at the top of its head, which was shaped like an isosceles triangle. They were light yellow, with a band of brownish green running through them. I could see the dragonfly was quivering, clinging to the bamboo with its tiny feet. Honami was barefoot as usual. The tips of her long toes looked completely drained of color. "That was so fast. A lot faster than I thought it would be." There was a quiver in Honami's voice, too. "He was hanging out near the surface, then, the next thing I knew, he was going up the bamboo . . . His back started bulging and, just like that, his skin split open. No, it didn't really split open . . . Mmm, more like it was being pushed apart from inside? Then his eyes and back came popping out . . . It was like the whole thing was on fast forward. So he started pulling himself out, shaking a little, or like, swinging himself from side to side . . . Then he did this thing where he curled backward and got his belly out, but the tip of his tail was still stuck, so he lunged forward, grabbed the bamboo, and yanked himself all the way out." I couldn't follow what Honami was saying. The dragonfly's wings were less crumpled now than when I first got there,

and its body was looking more opaque, more solid by the second, like it was hardening before our eyes. The green stripes looked sharper, too. As its wings continued to smooth out, they lost their color, becoming clearer, with thin black lines on them forming a neat grid of squares. Meanwhile, the shell appeared to be shriveling up. I could see a pair of white threads popping out of it. Maybe they're nerve fibers, I thought, connecting the shell and the insect inside. I'd seen cicada shells before with the same kind of threads. The dragonfly was trembling in the breeze. As it dried, everything stopped moving except its wings. One of the wings—the upper wing on the left side—looked like the others at the base but was crushed and twisted toward the tip. Something was definitely not the way it was supposed to be. Whatever the problem was, it looked like it might keep the dragonfly from being able to fly. An insect needs four wings and six legs. If it has to fly and one wing isn't right, it's going to have a real hard time. Maybe it won't be able to fly at all. Even if it can, it probably won't be able to fly well enough to hunt. If it's too slow or unsteady in the air, there's a good chance it'll end up getting devoured by some other dragonfly. "You can't keep one of these guys as a pet, can you?" Honami asked. "I wonder." "When he was a nymph, I gave him live snails, but what do you think he's going to eat as an adult? Flies? Ladybugs?" "Oh, maybe . . ." "What kind of cage would I need for that?" "Hmm . . ." "I know, it's not gonna work," she said. Then, as she tried to get up, she fell back on her butt. "Yeesh . . . Are your legs okay?" Honami asked. I stood up gingerly. My legs felt numb, but I managed. "I guess I'm not as young as I used to be," she said with a breathy laugh, getting up slowly with one hand on the pane of glass. "That wing . . . It's not in good shape, is it?" "Mmm . . ." "I was really hoping he'd turn out okay . . . Maybe the snails weren't enough?" "I don't think that was the problem . . ." "Maybe he needed more space. Or was he born that way? What if he got hurt when I caught him?" "Hmm." "Who knows, right? Well, I guess these things happen, even in nature . . ." "Definitely." "Anyway, he's a pretty one, isn't he?" We stood there until the blood came back to our legs. The dragonfly was perfectly still. The light of the sun was falling on its wings, casting a large latticed pattern on the aluminum-gray of the door frame.

When we went inside, Honami said it was time for lunch and made us some udon. It was already after eleven. "You okay with eggs?" "Um, uh-huh." "Raw eggs?" "Sure." On the noodles, we had egg, negi, tororo kombu, and wakame. "Tsukiyuki-san won't eat raw or soft-boiled eggs." "Really?" "You didn't know that?" "No." "Me neither—not until we got married." The white of the egg looked cooked, but when I touched it with my chopsticks I could tell it was pretty much raw inside. "This isn't going to be enough, is it? Not for a growing boy like you." "No, it's fine." "I only had two servings of noodles in the freezer." "This is plenty." "I'm really sorry about that . . ." Honami sprinkled her udon with a generous amount of shichimi, then got up without taking a bite and opened the curtains. I could see the strip of bamboo, and even though it was small I could see the yellow body on it. When Honami came back, she sat down next to me on the long side of the table and pulled her bowl over. "This way we can both see what he's up to." "Yeah." "Maybe he's a yellow waxtail." "Could be." "I mean, he's yellow." "Right." When we finished eating, Honami poured us some room-temperature mugicha. Sorry, she said, we don't have any ice. The escaped bits of egg white were floating around in my soup. I'd swallowed the barely warm yolk whole. Honami must have popped hers—her broth was cloudy. She asked if I was done, then took our bowls into the kitchen, rinsed them out, and washed her face. "I'm no good at eating noodles. It doesn't matter if it's udon or ramen, the soup always gets everywhere. It bugs me, so I have to wash my face when I'm done. That ever happen to you?" "Not really, I guess." "Seriously? Everybody says that . . . How do you keep the soup from flying all over the place?" After that, she wiped the table down with a cloth and said, "Okay, let's get started." Then she sat in her usual seat, with her back to the screen door.

It was hard to focus that day. I couldn't keep my eyes away from the damselfly. Every time Honami saw what I was doing, she twisted around to look, too. It was still there—in the same place. I have no idea how long it's supposed to take a damselfly to fly for the first time,
I thought, but with its wing that way, maybe it never will. Math, break, English. My mom had told me that Honami had spent some time with a family in America, but she said that wasn't true. "I've never even been there. She must have me confused with somebody else." "My mom can be a little scatterbrained," I said. "Moms always are. Even if they don't start out that way, it's how they end up. They have way too much going on." "You mean with raising kids?" "I mean with all of it." I had my eyes on my English workbook when Honami suddenly gasped. "He's gone!" I looked up and the damselfly was missing; the only thing there was the brown shell. We got up and opened the door. It really wasn't there. Honami stepped into her sandals and went into the yard. I went around to the front to get into my shoes. The shell looked even smaller than before—darker, too—with the same white threads popping out. We looked around, but it wasn't anywhere. "He did it! He flew!" "What a relief." "Tell me about it . . ." Honami said, still looking here and there. A breeze was blowing. In the neighbor's yard, the laundry was fluttering. The damselfly must have caught the wind and taken flight. Most of its wings were normal, and maybe that was good enough . . . We checked the screen door, then the wall between Honami's yard and the neighbor's, but the damselfly was nowhere to be found. Honami gently plucked the shell from the bamboo and said, "Something to remember him by." Then we went back inside and got to work. We were talking about my homework for the following week when my cousin came home. "I got us some cake . . . Who's hungry?" he said as he set a white box down on the table. He was wearing a suit this time, so he had to have been at work. "Cake!" Honami exclaimed as she burst into a smile. "To mark the occasion." "What's the occasion?" my cousin asked warily. "The flight of the damselfly. He finally molted—you *just* missed it." "Oh, wow," he said, then left, presumably to change clothes. On his way out, he said he wished he'd been there to see it. It almost sounded like he was reading the words off a prompter. Maybe Honami missed what he said, but she didn't respond; she headed straight for the kitchen with that same smile on her face and started boiling some water.

I got on my bike and went home. We'd started earlier than usual that day, so we finished early, too. In past weeks, every bike ride had ended with me drenched in sweat. That day, the breeze felt nice. I was in no rush, pedaling at a much slower pace than that morning. When I got home and grabbed my backpack out of the wire mesh basket, a flash of light caught my eye. It was the damselfly—flattened against the black fabric. The wings had come off the body and were stuck to the cloth. Its yellow body was twisted, the green stripes scrambled. Its delicate legs were all in pieces, pushed into the threads. The damaged part of the wing was missing. As carefully as I could, I pinched the damselfly's back, where it looked the strongest. I tried pulling it loose, but it was seriously stuck. Only the body came off; the head stayed put. The damselfly's jaws were clamped onto my bag. Its eyes were still bright. Beneath its transparent wings, the material of my backpack appeared just a little magnified.

When I went to my cousin's house the next Saturday, there was a small frame on the wall beside the monkey picture. It wasn't a drawing, though. It didn't look like a photo, either. When I got a little closer, I could see it was the molted skin of the damselfly mounted inside a deep black frame. The shriveled shell was curled to the left. "I went to buy a special box for it." During our lesson, a dot of light fell on the framed shell. The nymph cage had been put away. "Now all I have to figure out is how to get the ricefish through the winter . . ." I nodded. When I was about to start my last year of middle school, Honami got pregnant and our lessons came to an end. My mom said I should go to cram school so I could get into a good high school, and that's what I did. I heard my mom telling somebody on the phone how going with some random college grad didn't bring my grades up at all. Family or not, you have to get results, she said. I guess you get what you pay for, right? After Honami had the baby, my mom took me to my cousin's house so we could give them a present. The monkey picture wasn't there— neither was the nymph shell or the ricefish bowl. A pair of drying poles had been set up in the yard and were covered with underwear and towels. Maybe it was the wind, or maybe they were hung out that way to begin with, but some of the pieces of laundry were flipped over or lying on top of each other. When Honami showed me the baby, she said, "Sorry I couldn't stick with you through your exams." I still have the damsel-fly's triangular head. Its eyes are just as clear as they were, and when I look into them I can see a glint of light deep inside. 🐵

Kevin Brockmeier

Time as a Perpetual Motion Machine

THE MACHINE THAT SENT HIM TRAVELING back in time was not, in truth, a machine at all. It was an act of volition— the most abject and possibly the last act of volition to which he would ever lay claim. His life was a botch; at fifty, he could no longer deny it. More and more he found himself thinking about a particular August afternoon when he was eighteen years old and on the cusp of leaving home for college. The image was fixed in his mind like a photograph: a patch of green grass spotted with purple mint, diamonds of sky behind a chain-link fence, and him with his pool tan, healthy and strong, sitting in his backyard with the first girl he ever tried loving. Every night as he lay drifting off to sleep, and then again when he woke up, he saw it shining in his memory. Why was it, he thought, that you never stepped out of bed into the past, and always onto your dusty hardwood floor with that one loose board that clicked beneath your feet? He was fed up with it, with the missed chances, the slipups, his one-way march into the future, and so, one morning, he said enough.

It was like falling off a bicycle—one minute he was upright, proceeding forward through time, and the next he was on the ground. His eyesight was astonishing suddenly. So was his hearing. One two three he noticed a sprinkler discharging water somewhere, a car engine ticking as it cooled, the *pa-chip* of a goldfinch. Little green pinpricks of insects were hopping through the grass where he lay stretched back with his palms propping him up like a picnicker in a Manet painting. Not only that, but his girlfriend was reclining against him. He could smell her hair, see her impossibly white socks. He had done it.

In his fantasies, this was always the moment when he took her hands and disclosed the truth to her, overcoming her skepticism with his detailed knowledge of the future. He poised himself to make just such a confession. Instead, though, before he could speak, he heard himself saying, "Burgers or pizza?" exactly as he had the first time.

His girlfriend answered, "Either way, sugarplum." To hear her using his pet name again, "sugarplum," after so many years, made something billow inside him. "But," she said, "I only have ten dollars until Monday."

He tried once more, thinking, "I have something to tell you, something that might be literally unbelievable, but will you hear me out?" Again, though, his voice interrupted him: "I vote Wendy's, then."

Dammit, he thought, how weak-willed was he? *Say it,* he chastised himself, and he squeezed her shoulder, cleared his throat, and pronounced her name with a priest-like formality. But no: he didn't. Thirty-two years ago, at exactly this moment, he had sung a jingle from the Wendy's commercial, three little doo-woppy lines about biscuits, and that's what he did this time, too.

Then, in a rush of associative logic, he came to a desolating conclusion.

He had read a few books about time travel, attended a few lectures, and had a hobbyist's grasp of the science, so he understood the conundrum that venturing into the past presented. Displace so much as a molecule of oxygen, and the change would flourish and swell. Gradually, though not as gradually as you might think, that first submicroscopic discrepancy would alter the weather the whole planet over. Then, within days, weeks, or months, it would modify every subsequent process with any element of randomness or contingency, including, crucially, which of a man's 200 million sperm fused with his partner's egg at the moment of conception, and thus which children came into being, and thus the course of history. There was no such thing as a humble difference; every effect was a butterfly effect. The standard theory was that time travel, or at least time travel into the past, would always, by necessity, create an alternate timeline. He had just enough education to make sense of the idea; in truth, he was proud of himself for grasping it. Suddenly, though, as he kissed the back of his girlfriend's neck, breathing in her aroma of sunscreen and peppery sweat, and knit his hands together on her stomach so that he could feel it rising as she inhaled—all of it without his say-so—it occurred to him that maybe the world had only one timeline, its first, and that it could not be altered. Whatever groove his original decisions had cut was the groove they would inevitably follow. Every oxygen molecule had a predetermined path. There was no getaway.

Admittedly, the evidence was slim so far, and he had to allow he had never been known for his optimism. From inside himself, though, the conclusion seemed obvious, and this second-chance life of his quickly bore it out. He was an onlooker, a passenger. His choices kept happening without his permission; the world kept happening around him.

A few days after he rejoined the past, as he was setting off for college, he received a speeding ticket barely half a mile from home and called the officer "Your Honor," just as he had the first time. Sophomore year, he made a long-distance call and—dummy—broke up with his girlfriend. Then he drank himself black, just as he had the first time. He graduated, moved to DC, moved to Rochester. He saw the same movies, made the same mistakes. Wife number one and wife number two and a six-month pregnancy and zero children. His job at the restaurant, his job in health insurance, his string of jobs in real estate. Dental appointments and oil changes. Houses and apartments. Kidney stones, carcinomas, the misjudgments and the wasted years. Eventually, he began to look forward to the morning when he would wash back ashore in the present and wake up as he used to—without the slightest idea, that is, what might be coming next. The clock would move on; his life would resume. It was on its way, he thought. It would be here soon.

But when the morning arrived and at last he ventured out of bed, he found himself once again eighteen and wildly in love and the day felt like the deepest breath he had ever drawn.

The third time, like the second, was indistinguishable from the first. There it all was again, the sky, the sprinkler, the engine, and the goldfinch. The impossibly white socks. The green flecklike insects. Wives, jobs, illnesses, mistakes, and his twenties, his thirties, his forties, and fifty. And then the spring, and part of the summer, and that morning when the botch of his life finally became too much for him, and he stepped into the past, and the third time became the fourth.

The automation of the process, the efficiency, the way it transformed a lifetime's worth of free decisions into an organized system of belts and gear trains— that was why he called it the machine. Midway through the ninth repetition, however, he realized he was no longer thinking in such terms. The circle—that's what he was calling it now. Decades ago, centuries, he had stopped forming his thoughts as if he might be capable of speaking them. He knew better. Pretending he had someone to talk to was the purest make-believe. Mostly he regarded language as a kind of playscript now, enacted repeatedly down to the tiniest pause and syllable. However, from the rust-pile of words he'd retained, he found himself verbalizing a question: *When had it happened? When had the machine become a circle?* It had taken place subliminally, he was sure, well before he noticed it. Gradually, as he was concentrating on other things, he must have come to feel he was inhabiting a closed system, not just complete but ideal, abstract even. His predicament was a matter of geometry, not mechanics. Maybe his experiences concerned him, but they didn't actually need him. His first time through, he had occasionally felt that his life was trying to say something to him, a message coded in life's obscure braille of pattern and coincidence. If only he could decipher it, he told himself, everything would make sense. But the circle offered him no such thing. The circle did not communicate with him at all. A machine spoke to its purpose. A circle spoke only to itself.

By his inner math, he had spent more than three hundred years inside the circle. When you re-experience your life often enough, he had discovered, even the most colorless details begin to lock themselves in your memory—all those empty minutes spent brushing your teeth or trimming your nails or paying your bills or washing the dishes, the great inconsequentialia of your days, were immortalized in your mind like graduations or first kisses. There were fevers he anticipated with dread no matter how often they recurred, one-night stands and steak dinners he anticipated with want and hunger. But he couldn't deny the general blandness of his life. How many houses could you place on the market before your thoughts began to drift? How many dates could you have?

By the fifteenth time he found himself wishing he could flee his life for the past, wishing for it so forcefully that he actually succeeded, he had become eager for any moment, good or bad, that would seize his attention for a while. Orgasms, fistfights, and bouts of food poisoning. Drug trips, car accidents, and chiropractic adjustments. All that mattered was that they allowed him, temporarily, to forget the chain of decisions he was following, its sameness, its irrevocability.

At twenty-eight, and then again at forty, he had tried reading the King James Bible. Though he never made it further than Leviticus, and therefore never would, he was gradually, circle by circle, memorizing Genesis and Exodus. He understood no more than he ever had about God and death and what it all meant, but he could list the plagues and the commandments, could name the sons of Abraham, and early in his thirtieth go-round he was able to mark the day he caught up with Methuselah. Nine hundred sixty-nine years, he thought, and here I stand, none the wiser. He had learned only one thing: how quickly every-thing happened, and how quickly it happened again. The happiest moments of his life, the most ruinous, the most trivial—they were all like the second hand sweeping around the clock, returning to twelve with barely a pause. His girlfriend was answering, "Either way, sugarplum," his girlfriend was answer-ing, "Either way, sugarplum," and his girlfriend was answering, "Either way, sugarplum" again. Or he was watching a pair of raindrops race each other down the window of a hotel conference room, he was watch-ing a pair of raindrops race each other down the window of a hotel conference room, he was watching a pair of raindrops race each other down the window of a hotel conference room, and the left raindrop won. Or the child was dead, and so was the marriage, and he and his wife would not touch each other, he and his wife would not touch each other, he and his wife were crying and would not touch each other.

The calendar of his life kept ending and re-beginning. He could not change it. He had no prison wall or piece of chalk by which to tally up the years, and so eventually, as he knew he would, he lost count of them. He could sense his experiences becoming more and more abstract. He was like a tone sounding inside him-self, a bell, permeating each and every moment of his life. How many times had he rung out? he wondered. There must have been thousands of him in there, tens of thousands, abandoning the present again and again for that long-gone afternoon when he and his girlfriend were both eighteen, cheerful and strong and so prayerfully young, or rather she so prayerfully young and he looking like he was but gradually mummifying inside his costume of youth.

Had he known the repetitions to which time would expose him, everything might have turned out differently. Or perhaps not. In any case, it was too late to try again. 🐵

Haruki Murakami

———

The Zombie

translated by Jeffrey Angles

A MAN AND A WOMAN were walking down a road alongside a graveyard. It was late, almost the middle of the night. Mist hung in the air. No one would want to be walking in such a place at such an ungodly hour, much less the couple themselves, but unavoidable circumstances had brought them there. They held hands tightly as they hurried along.

"It's just like that Michael Jackson video," she said.

"Yeah, get ready for the gravestones to start moving," he said.

Right then they did hear a grating sound, as if something heavy was being moved. The couple stopped in their tracks and glanced at one another.

He smiled. "Don't worry. No reason to be so nervous. Must be some branches rubbing together or something. You know, just the wind."

But there was no wind. She held her breath and looked around. She felt terribly uneasy. She had a premonition that something bad—something evil—was about to happen.

A zombie.

But no, they didn't see anything. No sign of any dead bodies coming back to life. They started walking again.

She sensed his face stiffening. Strange.

Suddenly he blurted out, "Why are you walking in such a weird way? Doesn't look very nice."

"What? Me?" she asked in surprise. "Is there something strange about how I'm walking?"

"Yeah," he said. "It looks ridiculous."

"Really?"

"You look bowlegged."

She bit her lip. Sure, she might have a slight tendency to walk that way. She did tend to wear down the soles of her shoes on one side. Still, she didn't think that her odd gait was pronounced enough to draw such direct criticism.

She didn't respond. She was in love with him, and he loved her too. They were set to be married next month. It didn't make sense to get into a fight over something so trivial. Perhaps I am a little bowlegged, she thought, but who cares?

"This is the first time I've ever gone out with a bowlegged woman."

"Is that so?" she asked, forcing a smile. Is he drunk, I wonder? No, he hasn't had anything to drink tonight.

He continued, "And you've got three moles inside your ear, you know."

"Really? You're kidding. Which side?"

"The right. Just inside your right ear, three moles. They make you look really vulgar."

"You've got something against moles?"

"I've got something against vulgar-looking moles. I can't imagine anyone in the world would actually like them!"

She bit her lip even harder.

He continued. "And sometimes your armpits smell. If I'd met you in the summer, I'd never have gone out with you."

She sighed and let go of his hand.

"Hold on. Who do you think you are, saying stuff like that? You're being a jerk. You've never said such things before."

"I mean, even the collar of your blouse is dirty. The one you're wearing tonight—right now. Why're you such a slob? Can't you do anything right?"

She stayed silent. She was so angry she couldn't say a thing.

"Yeah, there're lots of things I've been wanting to point out. Your bowlegs, your body odor, your dirty collar, the moles in your ear—they're just the start. That reminds me, why do you wear those earrings? They don't look good on you at all. They make you look like a whore. No, actually, a whore would look sophisticated next to you. If you're going to wear earrings like that, you should put a ring in your nose too. It'd look great with that double chin of yours. Yeah, your double chin reminds me—your mother's a real pig. A swine through and through—oink, oink. That's what you're going to look like twenty years from now. Mother and daughter, both gluttons—just the same. Swine. You gobble your food down. And your dad's not much better. He can barely write a single kanji. The other day he wrote a letter to my parents, and they just made fun of him. His writing is atrocious. It's like he didn't even finish elementary school. What a family! No culture at all. Someone should pour gas on you all and light you up. I can just imagine your fat sizzling and burning."

"If you hate me so much, why are you marrying me?"

He ignored her, spitting out "Swine!" before going back on the attack. "And I haven't even started on your

privates. What a mess! I do it with you 'cause I have to, I guess, but you're like a cheap stretched-out rubber band down there. I'd die if that was me. If I was a woman with that thing, I'd be so embarrassed I'd die. Wouldn't matter how. I'd just be sure to kill myself right away. I'd be too embarrassed to live."

She stood there utterly dumbfounded. "I can't believe what you're saying . . ."

He suddenly grabbed his head in his hands. His face twisted as if he was in pain, and he fell to his knees. He tore at his temples with his nails. "My god, it hurts!" he shouted. "My head's about to split in two. I can't take it. The pain!"

She cried out, "Are you okay?"

"No, I'm not! I can't stand it. It's like my skin's on fire."

She put her hand on his face. It was hot, like he was burning up. She gently rubbed his cheeks and forehead. As she did, the skin sluffed off in thin layers, revealing the slick red flesh beneath. Her breath caught in her throat as she jumped back in horror.

He stood up. Then he began to grin. He began ripping away his skin with his own hands, peeling off one patch of flesh after another. His eyeballs dangled from their sockets. His nose was nothing more than two dark holes. His lips were gone, leaving two rows of teeth exposed in an ugly smirk.

"I got together with you just to eat your piggy flesh. What other reason could I possibly have to be with you? Unbelievable you never figured it out! You're such a moron! So stupid! A complete idiot!" And with that he let out an evil cackle.

The mass of exposed flesh started chasing her. She ran and ran, but no matter how hard she tried, she couldn't escape him. At the edge of the graveyard, his slimy hand grabbed hold of the collar of her blouse. She screamed for all she was worth.

THE MAN HELD HER in his arms.

Her throat was dry as a desert. He smiled and looked at her.

"What's the matter? Have a bad dream?"

She sat up and looked around. They were lying in bed in a lakeside hotel room. She shook her head awake. "Did I scream?"

"Did you ever!" He laughed. "You let out a really loud shriek. Everyone in the hotel probably heard. I hope they didn't think someone was being murdered."

"Sorry about that," she said.

"No big deal. Bad dream?"

"So bad, you have no idea."

"Want to tell me?"

"Not really," she said.

"You should talk about it. If you talk about it out loud, you'll get the bad vibes out of your system."

"It's okay. I don't want to talk about it right now."

They fell silent for a few moments. He wrapped his arm around her, holding her against his bare chest. They could hear the croaking of frogs in the distance. The man's heart thumped in his chest, sure, slow, and steady.

Something occurred to her. "Say, I want to ask you something."

"What?"

"Do I have any moles inside my ear?"

"Moles?" he responded. "You mean those three vulgar-looking moles inside your right ear?"

She closed her eyes. It was not over yet. 🐵

Mieko Kawakami

———

The Day Before

translated by Hitomi Yoshio

© Manny Trinh

In the forest where I go there is a cliff.
It started as a very low cliff,
so low you could easily make it to the bottom.
Then little by little the cliff got higher,
and then it got a bit lower,
then higher again.
Before long I would cower in fear just thinking about it.
One day not too far in the future
I might fall off the edge.
That's what I've been thinking these days.

Yesterday the cliff was higher again.
It's been like that lately,
getting higher every day.
I wonder why.
It happened little by little, then yesterday the cliff was suddenly enormous.
As if to cover it, cover everything above my head, the dark green swells and swells.
The forest and the cliff.

No one knows I go into the forest,
or maybe they're all just keeping quiet,
and they too go into the forest at night,
looking up at the swelling green perhaps.
I don't tell anyone about the forest,
but that's okay. I'm not lonely
since it must be the same for everyone.
Is there a cliff for them too?
Are they afraid
that one day they, too, will fall off the edge?

In my house Grandma has been sleeping for a very long time.
She was alive long before I was born, then we lived together,
and now she will die before me.
There is a bed
where Grandma sleeps
in the corner of an eight-mat tatami room.
The bed is big and electric and folds in the middle to lift her back, like this.
With all her brittle bones, she no longer walks, no longer talks,
but she's not ill.
She just sleeps, and while she sleeps her hair keeps growing.
Once every few months I take a pair of large silver scissors and cut her hair.
I cut and cut, but her hair grows and grows
until it covers her up,
covers her—up.

I feed her twice a day, the food all soft and mushy.
I slide a flat spoon gently between her lips,
then slip it all in at an angle—the mush that was resting on the round of the spoon.
The food and drink moisten Grandma's tongue
then glide down her throat and into her stomach unseen,
and the plastic bowl in my hand becomes lighter little by little,
one spoonful at a time.
The bowl becomes lighter so gradually that no one would notice.
The accumulating lightness
gives shape to what is called today,
gives—shape.

No one knows whether she is asleep or awake.
How long have I been looking at her?
How long have I been afraid?
Her arms resting alongside her body are thin and straight.
Her small hands, covered in wrinkles.
Her tanned skin—
for so many decades
the heat of the sun reached it.
No longer luminous, but the kind of skin you can feel without even touching.
Dark spots everywhere, sunken deep—
step into them and you'll never be able to extract your feet.
Her pale blue veins like thin lines drawn by a pen flow toward her fingertips,
or toward her heart underneath her pajamas, the gentle rise and fall of her chest.

What is it that flows in this body?
Or, what is it that doesn't flow there?
Cracked, tough, dried-up, yet soft,
the gutters of her skin that long ago held a vital force.
Her chin no longer has excess flesh.
Protruding,
her jawbone gaunt.
I look.
In my eyes they become bigger,
in my eyes they become bigger and bigger.

In my eyes, Grandma is enormous. She becomes the place where not a single
   person remains.

When I descend there is no one in sight.
One moment the ground is parched dry—then the mud comes sliding along,
preventing me from moving forward.
I have nowhere I need to go,
but I can't just keep standing still.

No one is here,
but all around me there are traces of digging.
The unearthed dirt is a little damp,
as if someone was here only a moment ago, digging up the dirt, like this.
You dig and dig, but your hands find nothing.
The sweat falls into your eyes.
Your arms and fingers grow numb.
You no longer remember what it was you're digging for.
So it seems that someone was digging the dirt here, like this,
looking for something.

Only five centimeters deeper, three minutes more,
and maybe,
just maybe, you'll find something that would make things go back to the way they were.
At night all alone,
terrified that you stopped—just there—yet again.
There.
It could have been right there.
So it seems that someone was here, like this,
digging for something.

I stand looking at what remains of the dirt.
Then I realize
that it is all beginning to overflow.
As if something is falling from the sky, as if something is starting to shine,
brimming over from underneath my feet.
They are the ringtones of countless cellphones,
countless phones ringing—resounding—reverberating.
Music, melodies, bells, chimes, ringing tinkling
merging resounding
glittering sparkling—
falling from the sky like golden droplets of rain
on a sunny day.

No one is here,
Not a single person remains in this place.
It's all dried up, and soon it will no longer exist.
They've all been washed away,
And yet people are ringing, calling out to who knows whom.
Don't they know?
Perhaps they don't know.
Right.
Just like those who are no longer here
didn't know that they would be gone tomorrow.
The day before they were gone.
Yes
We are all living in the day before—
not knowing, not ever knowing
what will happen tomorrow.

The cliff is higher again today.
Turning my head from the abyss, I pretend I am swimming.
The forest and the cliff.
The cliff is higher.
Rising up and down faintly as if breathing, it becomes higher then lower,
then higher again.
The forest covers the sky,
covers—the sky.

Today is the day before.
Today is—the day before.
Perhaps, today is the day before.
Think of this:
In the space between living and dying
lies Grandma sleeping.
She fed me until my body grew this big.
Into my newly formed mouth barely open
she would slide in a flat spoon gently,
then slip it all in at an angle.
The mush that was resting on the round of the spoon.
Grandma will die along with all the memories and whatever else.
Today is perhaps
the day before.
Perhaps we all live in—the day before.
I look upon her face,
wanting to capture the space between living and dying.
How long have I been looking
at her skin and what seems to lie beyond?

In the forest where I go there is a cliff.
It started as a very low cliff,
so low you could easily make it to the bottom.
Then little by little the cliff got higher.
Before long I would cower in fear just thinking about it.
One day not too far in the future
I might fall off the edge.
That's what I've been thinking these days.

The world
is filled with
the day before.
The forest swells,
the cliff surges.
How can we put an end to this?
How can we eliminate from this world
the day before?

I go to the forest and stand at the edge of the cliff.
If I can annihilate my own day before,
then perhaps—the day before—will be gone forever.

The wind blows, filling my blouse like a sail, and I straighten up, close my eyes,
    and jump.
My body is sucked to the ground as I fall into the abyss—yes, I fall and fall.
And just as my body is dashed to the ground,
I am standing once again at the edge of the cliff.
I take a deep breath, close my eyes, and kick off the edge, kicking off as hard as
    I can with my heels.
And just as my body is dashed to the ground, I am standing at the edge of the cliff,
    standing once again.
I kick off the edge to put an end to the day before. I land on her skin. I run across
    the surface, I leap over the veins that will soon stop flowing. I kick off her chin
    and fall once again.
I fall, yet the moment I am dashed to the ground I am standing once again
    on the cliff. I am standing on the cliff I am standing on the cliff I am standing
    at the edge of her chin. My back moist from the warm breeze, I stand firm,
    flexing my calves, and when I turn around the forest stretches out, the forest
    swells and swells.
The forest swells. I try to cut, but my scissors are no longer here, my scissors are
    no longer, no longer.
The day before, I am standing on the cliff, I kick off the edge I kick off the edge
    I kick off.
The forest—and—the cliff.

Whether Grandma is asleep or awake, no one knows.

How long have I been looking at her?

Today is—the day before.

The forest and the cliff.

Note from the translator: This poem was published in 2013, two years after the Great East Japan Earthquake (3.11; the 2011 Tohoku earthquake and tsunami). The Japanese theater company Mum & Gypsy performed an excerpt from this poem during the closing event of the 2014 Tokyo International Literary Festival. After the festival, they toured to Nagano, Kyoto, Osaka, Kumamoto, and Okinawa. A translation of that excerpt was published in *Wasafiri 102: Japan: Literatures of Remembering* (2020).

© Satoshi Kitamura

Music
A Monkey's Dozen

Unlike a baker's dozen (one extra!), a monkey's dozen is one short. In this section you will find eleven stories, poems, a Noh play, and graphic vignettes that feature music— the special focus of this volume.

© Sara Wong / TOOGL

Aoko Matsuda

———

Angels and Electricity

translated by Polly Barton

THE CARD EMERGED FROM the envelope along with a handful of two-dollar bills. The faded envelope was lilac in color, and on it my name, written out in the English alphabet, had been scrawled in ink of a similar shade. Both lilacs had once been brighter.

On the front of the card was a unicorn with peculiarly long eyelashes, together with a blonde angel, a rainbow arching across a blue sky in the background. The image was dotted with glittery patches, which felt strange to the touch. It wasn't just the glitter that gave the card its strange texture, though. Noticing the lumpy bit in the bottom left corner, I recalled what had happened when I'd first opened it.

I hadn't known what was going on. After a moment, it came to me that I was hearing an odd noise that could only be described as electronic, and then I realized that the noise was coming from the card in my hands. Peals of warm-sounding laughter rose up among the adults sitting around the table. So distracted was I by the card's jittery sound that I couldn't take in the message written inside it—couldn't take in those lilac words commemorating my seventeenth birthday. The melody was like a mosquito flying around the room, oblivious to the person frantically chasing it, which made it hard for me to think of anything else. Still in that state, I opened the long thin envelope inside the card to find five pristine two-dollar bills.

"I thought they were kind of unusual," said a voice in hesitant Japanese from the end of the table. The voice was Yuka's.

Yuka must have been in her mid-twenties then. Born and brought up in the US, she'd learned Japanese at Sunday school from an early age, and her parents spoke Japanese almost exclusively at home, so her mastery of the language was decent enough. Yet when she spoke Japanese, Yuka—who held a demanding job in an IT firm—would instantly take on the air of a diffident child. Partly due to that, partly due to how I was back then, not to mention some other factors as well, there was always a certain tension when the two of us conversed, and time didn't flow by smoothly.

"Thank you," I said, just as hesitantly, without looking at her, and closed the card. I was relieved to hear the strange electronic sound stop.

It wasn't until the plates were being cleared away with a clatter—plates we'd used for the slices of pastel-colored birthday cake, which seemed to originate from the same world as the unicorn and the angel—that I finally realized the card was playing "Over the Rainbow," the song that Dorothy sings in *The Wizard of Oz*.

I loved the greeting card aisle in American supermarkets, but I wasn't so keen on these musical cards. Their lackluster electronic melodies left me unsettled, and I didn't understand the need to take lovely tunes and deliberately reproduce them in such an odd format. I felt the same about the music that they played in supermarkets and dentists' waiting rooms—all kinds of well-known songs that had been transformed, via some kind of magic the world never wanted or needed, into music-box versions. Then there was the way that the music-producing device made one part of the card thicker than the rest. I didn't like how, when you put one of those musical cards in a pile with other cards, it alone would stick right out. That was exactly what had happened just now, in fact: when I removed the stack of cards dug out from an old cardboard box, this one seemed different from the rest. That was why I'd picked it up.

Come to think of it, it was possible that back then, I'd listened to that cheap version of "Over the Rainbow" only that one time. In other words, I'd only ever opened the card that once.

Now when I opened the card, whose corners had faded to white, I found myself listening intently. I couldn't hear a thing. Of course I couldn't: over a decade had elapsed. Inside the card—with its picture of flowers with faces and a picket fence, as well as a ribbon blowing in the wind whose connection to the rest of the scene was hard to fathom—was a message written in lilac ink:

"Happy birthday! Enjoy being 17!"

I stared at that short message in English as if seeing it for the first time. It was hard to believe that there'd been a moment when this card had borne some relation to me.

"Pfffff. Enjoy being 17, my ass! Right?"

A voice was speaking to me. I felt my whole body stiffen. Was this apartment that I'd just moved into haunted? It was built just five years back, and had no tatami flooring, which was clearly the favored environment for ghosts. Nor did it have cupboards with the conventional sliding doors, but rather the kind of walk-in closet I'd always dreamed of. Wasn't five years a bit short for it to have acquired a resident spirit? Gathering up my courage, I was about to turn round and look, when the voice said,

"It's been a while, eh, Michiru?"

It was a voice I'd heard somewhere before. I didn't need to scrabble around in my mental drawers for where, because the answer lay in my hands. The voice speaking to me was Yuka's.

"Yuka . . ." I murmured.

"Yep!" the voice replied, brightly.

"Are you—dead?" I addressed the card in my hands, in a manner that could only be described as idiotic.

"No, no! I'm not dead," came the cheerful reply. I felt as though I could see Yuka waving her hand in front of her face, as if to bat away my suspicions.

"So what's the deal with this supernatural stuff, then?"

"I don't really know, to be honest, but I get the feeling that I'm the part of Yuka that she usually neglects. The real Yuka is slaving away at the office as we speak. She really is a textbook workaholic."

"This Yuka's Japanese is really good!"

"Yeah, because I'm like a conceptual Yuka. Real Yuka's Japanese is only getting worse. Back then, there was you and the other kids who'd come over from Japan, but there's not a lot of that anymore, so there's not much opportunity for her to use it. Mom and Dad are really disappointed. They feel like all their efforts have come to nothing."

Yuka's parents had taken in overseas students from Japan out of choice. Yuka's mom was particularly enthusiastic about the whole thing, volunteering as an ikebana teacher to promote Japanese culture. She had created a community of Japanese people and those interested in all things Japan who lived locally. I'd learned the hard way that you had to be careful of said community. If you weren't quick to say no, you could get roped into going along to their weird Japan festivals and stuff. Not just going, either, but going in a kimono—an overly short kimono with a strange pattern that somebody must have left in the house at some point. Photographic evidence of such occurrences is probably nestled somewhere in the same cardboard box where I found that bundle of cards. I had no desire to be confronted by it.

Yuka kept herself apart from all of that—the endless stream of kids arriving from Japan, and her mother's unstinting devotion to run around after them. Whenever Yuka was at home, her mother would try to persuade her to do things for us, so she stayed out as much as possible.

I say "us," but the line-up of faces was constantly in flux. There were various types of visitors, from those who just wanted to experience life in the US, staying just a few weeks before going back, to those who'd stay with Yuka's family before moving into their school dorms. They all had some kind of "situation" back in Japan, and they all had parents with sufficient money to send them overseas.

Sometimes Yuka would be unable to refuse her mother's entreaties and would take us to a movie on Saturday night.

Yuka didn't talk much, and she never invited us into her room, which was in a separate part of the house, so I didn't really know what kind of person she was, but getting into her car I felt like I'd been allowed inside her bedroom. I don't recall even vaguely what model of car it was or its color, but I can remember the little details of that small room even now. That cardboard lemon hanging from the rearview mirror, which smelled—surprise, surprise—of lemon. In the space between the back seat with its two little cushions and the rear window was a box of Kleenex, which would slide back and forth every time Yuka braked. Why do tissue boxes kept in cars always look so floppy and lifeless? Is it because they're out there exposed to the sun all day?

Yuka wasn't the type to have the radio on, and instead kept several CDs stashed in her car. When we piled into the back, she would slide one she'd picked at random into the car stereo. On the rare occasions when we showed an interest and found one we wanted to listen to, she'd put it on for us, looking not totally displeased. Rickie Lee Jones, Juliana Hatfield, Eddi Reader, Lisa Loeb—Yuka liked female singers

with sugary voices. One day, when I was back in Japan and was browsing through Tower Records, I felt myself pinned by a gaze coming from a CD on the rack: it was the red-haired woman with glasses, half of whose face appears on the cover of *Angels & Electricity*. Recognizing it as one of the albums that had been in Yuka's car, I bought it. Even now, whenever I'm in a shop or convenience store and hear a foreign woman singing in dulcet tones, it occurs to me that that very song might be playing at this moment in Yuka's car. Yuka always wound down her window all the way, letting her long hair be whipped about by the wind. At the Baskin-Robbins where we'd stop on the way home, I always ordered a double scoop of mint chocolate chip, and she'd look at me with distaste.

"Did your English improve after I last saw you?"

It began to seem perfectly normal that Yuka was speaking to me like this.

"Not at all! I barely use it here. There were quite a few Japanese kids at my high school in the States, and I came back to Japan as soon as I graduated."

As I answered, I pressed on the front of the card that had once played "Over the Rainbow," trying to figure out what was going on, but my prodding didn't provide any clues. It was just an old greeting card.

"Well, I guess your reason for coming in the first place wasn't to learn English."

With that one remark, I instantly felt my reality growing distant. Of course, you might ask what right I have to speak of reality when I'm hearing a voice coming from a greeting card, so instead, let's say the thread that held me and reality together was severed even more definitively. Every time I recall that period, I have to tie the pieces together again. It's bizarre how many times that piece of thread can be cut. However old I get, however much I try to reinforce it, it makes no difference.

I'd stabbed someone. Back in my last year of junior high. Having fallen for a classmate who was a bit of bad boy, I made the decision to turn bad myself. In the small town where I lived, turning bad was ever so easy. I became a bad girl, and so I got with the bad boy, but he turned out to be a bit of a player, and I went a bit funny in the head, and I slashed the arm of one of my rivals with a box cutter. Needless to say, she bled.

Seeing the blood, I became lightheaded and fainted, and my rival ended up rousing me and helped me up, asking, "Are you okay?" In other words, a truly messed-up situation. Because she said she wasn't badly hurt, and because everyone involved was clearly from the wrong side of the tracks, nothing particularly bad came of it, but my parents, their nerves well and truly frayed, used their connections to find Yuka's parents, and I was flown to the US. I'm still terrified of that funny-in-the-head girl from back then. I still remember that muddled, hotheaded feeling, as though my brain were on fire. If that me ever rocks up again, it really will be game over.

"You had such a dark look about you back then. I remember when you'd been here for about a year, we watched *The Wizard of Oz* on TV. You sat there watching the whole thing with no expression at all, but then right at the end you suddenly burst into tears. I remember thinking what a creepy kid you were."

"Wow, this Yuka is really mean!" Even as I said these words, I was surprised to notice that the black mist that had descended across my mind as we'd been talking had suddenly cleared. Being told so lightheartedly that I was creepy made my memories from that time, which I'd been brooding on for so long, feel lighter, too.

"Which is why I want to say to myself, you can't go saying to a kid with all that darkness in their eyes, 'Enjoy being 17!' I guess you were crying because, after being whisked off to the US yourself, you identified with Dorothy being whisked off by a tornado, right? And when she said 'There's no place like home!' it made you tear up. All of which makes the choice of the song in the card really bad. I guess I just picked it because I thought you liked *The Wizard of Oz*. To try to tell you that, like, you might have darkness in your eyes now but some day you'll make it over the rainbow. Although it's also possible that I didn't actually think about any of that . . ."

It was true that I really liked *The Wizard of Oz,* but I didn't identify with Dorothy. I'd cried because I was drawn in by the simple sweetness of that world where Judy Garland sings in a sugary voice about a land she dreams of over the rainbow, and then, once the adventure is over, utters that iconic line, "There's no

place like home!" and goes back to Kansas. In other words, it worked on me in the very standard way that films and music and stories work on people, and had nothing to do with my real-life self.

At that time, my real-life self was the epitome of dullness. I was discovering back then that being Asian was no longer a unique selling point—it didn't make me particularly stand out. The US, too, turned out to be different from how I'd imagined. The high school I was sent to didn't have the kind of rigid social pecking order that was always there in the high school movies I'd watched back in Japan, and it didn't have a football team either. And no team meant no cheerleaders— in other words, nobody stood out. Everything was dull, and I felt like I'd been scammed. I didn't love Japan enough to think that home was best, but I didn't fall for the US either. They were equally unspectacular.

One thing that did take me by surprise about the US was that there were moments when, if you weren't asserting yourself, then it was as if you didn't exist. You were there, but you weren't. What kind of eyes did American people have, to see things that way? In Japan, however quiet you were, it never caused you to disappear. So long as you were physically present, you'd be counted. The feeling that my own contours had vanished was new to me. In one way it seemed cruel, but at the same time the sensation was kind of pleasurable. It was like I'd become one of those invisible characters from sci-fi movies.

"It sounds like my parents are still in touch with yours," Yuka said.

Yuka's parents visited Japan every three or four years, and each time, my parents would put together a whole program of entertainment for them. As long as they lived, they would never forget their debt to this couple who'd helped reform their delinquent only daughter. Had I been reformed, though? During my three-year stay in the US I reverted to a calmer version of myself, but that didn't mean I'd become more positive or felt better. It was rather that I'd sort of realized that everywhere was the same, and given up as a result. I'd left home and didn't see Yuka's parents as much as my mom and dad did, but the times we'd occasionally meet, and the two of them would see me holding down a normal sort of job, dressed in a beige suit and tights with a black bob, they'd make a big song and dance of how delighted they were. After all, when I'd shown up at San Francisco Airport, with bright-red blush on my cheeks and long permed hair, I was the textbook image of a dropout. So predictable.

Yuka's parents liberally sprinkled their Japanese sentences with English nouns: "Is that temple the one on the *riverside*?" "It's got such beautiful *straight-lines*." Listening to them chattering away like this as they happily chowed down their Japanese food, it struck me just how far away the US had become for me.

"Hey, this is just a hunch, but did your mom used to lie about stuff?"

All of a sudden I found this thing, which I'd never spoken to anybody about, spilling from my mouth.

"Oh my god, you noticed that too?"

One day when I came home from school—I guess it was shortly before my seventeenth birthday—Yuka's mom intercepted me, a serious expression on her face. There was nobody else in the house. I sat down in the small built-in dining space in a corner of the kitchen, as I was invited to do, and then she began talking to me in her normal friendly voice, "You know, yesterday evening, Yuka suddenly broke down in tears and told me that she's convinced that you hate her. She says she can tell, by the way you act toward her."

You know how it is with her, she went on to say, She's not very expressive when it comes to her feelings, and she must have been holding it in, the poor thing, it makes me feel so sad. Oh, I'm sorry to do this, but you must make an effort to be kind to her from now on, okay, Michiru? As she was talking, Yuka's mom's own feelings seemed to get the better of her and she burst out crying herself. Taken aback, I apologized, but she said, as she wiped her tears, No no, it's okay, Michiru, don't apologize. Then smiling bravely she said, It's okay, you can go now, and handed me a plate with a homemade cookie on it.

Returning to my room, I ate the cookie with brightly colored M&Ms baked into it in a state of shock. I hadn't done anything particularly nasty to Yuka, but considering my default mode of behavior at that time, it wouldn't have been particularly strange for someone to have the impression that I disliked them. Along-side the guilt I felt, I was sickened by the idea that she

would go and tell on me like that. I felt as if my whole body had been infected by someone else's animosity and had turned pitch black. Which was why it was so unexpected when Yuka gave me that card for my birthday, and why I'd not been able to say thank you properly. I didn't know what to do, and as time went by even more distance opened between us, and then I went back to Japan.

It was last year that it came to me, à propos of nothing, that it had been a lie. I'd forgotten about the incident entirely, but something trivial had brought it to mind, and thinking it over, the adult me instantly smelled a rat. Yuka's behavior hadn't changed in the slightest around the time Yuka's mom made her shock-ing confession, and she had never taken that much interest in me to begin with.

"There were things that happened back then that I found really weird, like the way a certain kid in the house would suddenly start looking at me with this terrified look in their eyes. When I refused my mom's requests for help, her eyes would take on this strange glint, which scared me. I think she was fed up with how I was refusing to have anything to do with the whole enterprise, when she was doing so much. I guess the lying provided a kind of outlet for her. But it's not cool to do that to children—in fact, it's pretty worrying behavior. I have a feeling it was restricted to that period of time, though. She was just generally acting weird back then," Yuka said, a troubled expression on her face.

"Thinking about people's animosity way after the fact, it all seems so petty, doesn't it?" I put into words the feeling I'd had when I remembered the incident the previous year.

"Wow, how very grown up of you," Yuka said, affecting amazement. Embarrassed, I looked down at the card and glimpsed the pile of two-dollar bills. When I told her that I'd never actually used them, she replied, again in an affected tone, "No way! What a blow!"

To tell the truth, I hadn't known what to do with them. I felt that if two-dollar bills were such a rarity, then I should probably hold on to them, and I wondered self-consciously about what I'd do if I went to use them in a shop and the clerk remarked on the fact I was using two-dollar bills, and so I ended up never using them. I had the feeling that even if I were to go to the US in the future, I still wouldn't use them.

"Do you know they printed a 2,000-yen note in Japan as well, but it fell out of use very quickly?"

"Is money with two in it considered inauspicious?"

"Hey, inauspicious is a big word! This Yuka really is different."

"Shut up! Don't you think they should have thought about the fact that it had gone so wrong in the US before they printed 2,000-yen notes in Japan?"

"I guess they just thought, well, it's *our* country, so it'll be fine."

Talking about inconsequential stuff like this, half an hour passed in a blink. At some point, Yuka's voice began to grow crackly and cut out intermittently.

"This battery thing that isn't a battery is really quick to run out, isn't it?" I said. Yuka made hmmm, and then said, "Maybe I'm allowed to talk to you for the exact amount of time that Yuka spent thinking about you in the last ten years. Maybe that amount of time is tracked inside the card just like battery power."

She might be right, I thought, and then . . . only thirty minutes over the course of ten years? It didn't sound like much. But when I thought about it as meaning that Yuka had sometimes remembered me, when throughout she'd maintained the attitude that those Japanese kids in her house had nothing to do with her, it actually seemed like a lot, and I also felt that reducing this extraordinary experience that allowed me to speak to her to just its length in minutes was wrong, somehow.

"You should remember me much more than that! What a cold-hearted woman you are," I said laughing.

"Sorry! But that's how Yuka is, you know? She's not a bad egg, though. You should send her a text now and then, when you've got the chance. Right. For my finale, I'm going to sing for you. *Somewhereeeee ooooooover the rainbowwww . . .*"

The sweet-toned female voice cut out, and the room returned to silence. I was alone again in my apartment. I tried opening and closing the card a bunch of times, knowing full well it was useless. In my hands was just another infantile greeting card in assorted pastel colors.

For two weeks I continued opening and closing the card whenever the thought struck me, and then I stumbled across an online ad with the slogan *I Fix All Standard Electronic Devices!* So I took it in to the shop.

A week later, sitting in a park not far from the electronics shop, I opened the card. Beneath a blue sky, that stupid jittery "Over the Rainbow" began to play. I could no longer hear Yuka's voice.

Even through my slight horror at encountering that horrendous electronic noise again, I knew that there would be a time when I needed it. Yuka had been my first ever DJ. Whenever I felt like I might be approaching the edge, nearing the game-over point again, all I'd have to do was open this card. I had faith that if that ever happened, this special number selected for me by DJ Yuka would save me. 🐵

Hideo Furukawa

Heavensound

translated by Kendall Heitzman

© Keisuke Kondo

INTRODUCTION

JAPANESE PUBLISHERS LARGE AND SMALL responded to the Covid-19 pandemic at a speed the English-speaking world could only dream of, and Furukawa Hideo's *Ten'on* (Heavensound) is no exception. Only a little over five months elapsed between the last event mentioned by date in this epic poem (the speaker's arrival in Italy on June 15, 2022) and its publication in book form, on November 22, 2022.

Furukawa's first poetic endeavor is fraught with double meanings and neologisms, nowhere more so than in the name of the title concept-turned-persona, 天音 Ten'on, "heaven's sound" or "heaven's music," a homonym for 天恩 *ten'on,* "heavenly blessings," and here rendered as Heavensound. The character 音 appears in words such as 音符 (*onpu,* "musical notes"), here rendered as "gracenotes" to signify that this otherwise ordinary word has been sanctified by virtue of the character it shares with 天音 (technically, they are not "grace notes" in the common English meaning, but they do borrow a certain ephemerality from the association). In many cases, the repetition of characters, impossible to duplicate in English, has shifted into other forms of poetic play: rhymes (and sight rhymes and slant rhymes), assonance, alliteration, and homonyms all point to the presence of something in the original.

As the world begins to open up—more quickly than Japan reopens to the world—the speaker encounters the Heavensound, the sound of the Japanese language, in an unexpected way: by flying from Japan to California. Heavensound as a concept and as a poem wanders across major cosmologies, including Shinto, Buddhism, and even the mythos of America. Everywhere it goes, it invokes symbols of the oppressed: minor dialects of Japanese, the horseshoe crabs that gave their blue blood for vaccine research, and—in part V, the section that appears here in translation—the umbrellas of recent Hong Kong protests. Here, the speaker finds himself in a sort of underworld, playing the part of an Orpheus or Dante. Furukawa has said that the *Divine Comedy* is a vital touchstone for his writing.

And now, let us reverberate!

Wandering Heavensound
and this, a record of the dream
with which I was entrusted   personally
I awoke the Heavensound from its nightmares
the frightening dream   that the Heavensound saw
it had become melodyroots, fluting underground
to support the rhythmstalk and harmonyleaves
but something was twisted
its vowels couldn't burrow through the rock-riddled furrow
its consonants
couldn't seep through the sure steel slabs
this was the death of poetry
and then the very cells of the melodyroots, the gracenotes,
were carried from their clefs by the underground streams
by the rivers that flow in the clefts between the layers
The byways of America are the waterways of America,
I said earlier, but
the subterranean streams are a stratum of repression on the World
in that dark network of waterways
the vowels tried all at once to open their umbrellas
the Heavensound saw   that valiant fight
their terrible struggle
it saw the flames
and if   this happened to be hell   then those were the fires of hell
Hellfire is the name of a missile, you know
the one narrating this   was me
not the Heavensound
it was listening, the Heavensound was listening
to the warp of the Canopy Symphony
the screech
the tilt
How could it do otherwise?   with the withering of the rhythmstalk
and the leavetaking of the harmonyleaves
comes the deep sleep of the sym   pho   ny—
no!
Even should you become the king of discord,
you must live!
Heavensound hollered
and I shouted with it
Where is the portal?
the one to ask this   was me
Tell me   where is the passage from the underground?

the one to ask this   was me
then I saw it   at the shore of the subterranean lake—a stage
someone had set up a stage
"In *this* World, we are all equally blind!
(La-di-da-di-da!)" a singer in sunglasses,
whirling his long hair, warbled
well, who did we have here
if it wasn't inspiration incarnate
Mister or maybe Miz Inspiration,
where is the portal?
That's me, again

    Don't lose the track now, record of my travel!
    Find the way back now, poem, don't unravel!

a way, aweigh   said the Heavensound
the Heavensound saw   the frenzied melody   had been reborn as a symphonic bouquet
claimed by a melodious machine
and the machine was operated by   doves
a pair of turtledoves, above
the underground is no place for their kind
Their habitat is the Surface
and the hand of deliverance will come from there
O deliverance! O salvation!
and there,
and then, it is curtains-up on the turtledove opera
Wandering Heavensound
this pair of turtledoves lives in the great forest
the space between the trees, measured in millimeters, is suffused with opera
the gathering of vegetation, measured in light years
the photons and electrons absorb the singing
"There is no place that you can call *here*"
a declaration perfectly encapsulated
in the prayer
Hail, Amitabha Buddha
the opera gallops down a slope, to the low places on the Surface
the Heavensound said And now, down to *that* World!
I could see   that the Heavensound had been revived

                        and cried,

    gracenotes,   you have resolved the mystery of the quanta
    gracenotes,   you have burned up every last bit of oxygen
    gracenotes,   you have sought not musical staves but arboreal spaces
    the mysterium of Flora
    the blood vessels in the Space between trunk and limbs
    the refrain scored on veins   the filial pedigrees of arteries
    the Time brought into this world   by the gracenotes

And now the runway
Today, June 14, 2022   Tuesday   Japan Standard Time for just a little longer
I have come to Hane/da, the field of wings

What if we put it like this?
The tale I tell of myself has nothing to do with the imbroglios of the Japanese archipelago,
                                                                    or should I say,
The tale I tell of myself is on the same page as the Japanese language.

Beloved, let us reverberate!

© Sam Messer

Kaori Fujino

———

Transformers: Pianos

translated by Laurel Taylor

I THINK SOMETIMES THINGS just don't work out. If they did, people like me and my sister would have gotten the short end of the stick. Or people like my mom.

My sister says, "Pianos aren't very smart, are they?" But maybe we have the wrong idea.

THE PIANOS ARE BITING BACK. They've decided to start a war with humanity. Why would they do something like that, you ask. Isn't it obvious? For revenge.

Me and my sister have this idea that up till now the pianos have had to put up with all sorts of things. Take our family piano, for example.

Our upright used to be Mom's. Our great-grandfather bought it for her when she was little. He had this idea that proper young ladies should learn piano.

But Mom isn't a proper young lady, and she didn't have any talent for piano. Me and my sister know. Mom is completely tone deaf. You wouldn't know it from the way she talks, but when she sings, her voice can never settle on a note, it's all over the place. Like this tanker truck I saw in a movie once, when its tires skidded. No sense of rhythm either. She mows down pickup notes, triple meter, semitones, and more, sweeping everything along by force. By the time she's done singing, all the rules have lost meaning and been bowled down into a giant hole made specifically for their disposal, and there they wait to be buried.

A person like that could never play piano. But in spite of this, Mom went to lessons for five whole years before she quit. The keyboard lid stayed closed, gathering piles of dust, dictionaries, and textbooks. Every now and then a stray cat snuck in and sprawled on top of the piano.

The situation only got worse once me and my sister started to play.

Neither of us is tone deaf, but we grew up hearing Mom's lullabies and humming, so any piano talent we ever had was burned to a crisp long ago.

Even so, Mom brought the piano from her parents' house and enshrined it on a carpet in the narrow tatami room in our apartment. She said she thought it would be cute to see us two little girls playing duets. In matching poofy white dresses with ribbons tied at our waists. The ribbon would be . . . let's see, a more mature blue for you, pink for your sister.

"Do you want to play piano?" she asked.

"Yeah!" we answered. The dresses had us hooked.

Mom took immediate action. We only found out we'd actually been enrolled in piano lessons after all the paperwork was already done. For a while, Mom held on to the hope that at least one of us would become a professional pianist.

Every day me and my sister were chased into the tatami room and forced to practice. I was especially bad. Mom ordered me to make sure my sister practiced an hour first before taking another full hour to practice myself. Once my sister started school, it was also my job to make her run back home without any dawdling.

My sister sucked. She had no desire to improve, and she hated playing, so being terrible didn't bother her. She didn't play with her fingertips—instead she pushed the keys with the pads of her fingers full on the ivories, even though the teacher told her over and over to stop. She also played using the outside edges of her pinky fingers, which made her soft toddler bones curl inward. This bothered Mom, who started trying to pinch those fingers flat whenever we were watching TV, but even that didn't bother my sister. What did bother her was me giving her orders about anything and everything.

The second her fingers stumbled, I shouted, "Wrong!" I'd push her aside and sit on the bench, show her how to play the spot the right way, and then go even further, playing more and more of what came next. I hated piano too, but I was desperate to get good enough to make a fool out of her. I usually managed to play with the proper form, and my pinkies were thicker and stronger than hers, so they stayed straight and beautiful.

I never knew the joy of music. But in those moments I loved it, loved the piano.

Playing through my sister's tantrums, all her screeching and blubbering, felt absurdly good. It was different from when I was just practicing or playing for my teacher. In order to defeat my sister's wailing, my body knew what it had to do. I obeyed with pleasure, letting everything ripple down my two arms through my elbows and out. When I did, my fingers transferred all that power to the keyboard, and the keys responded by sinking down deeper than ever. I felt the melody twine around my own muscles. I felt the rhythm squeeze my muscles until they tingled.

Of course my happiness didn't last long. Just a moment, really.

Soon enough, my sister, snot dripping from her nose, would grab at me or the keyboard. She'd wrap herself around my waist and drag me off the bench or throw herself at the keys, sending up sounds almost like modern music. I kicked at her as I kept trying to play with all my might, but in the end our fingers wound up being used to push and pull at shoulders or chests or hair, and we made a fitful racket as the piano was battered by heads, jaws, elbows, and sometimes even knees.

And this wasn't our only attack on the piano. It was still in danger even when me and my sister were getting along or when we were facing off with the piano one-on-one.

We'd sit on top of the keyboard lid. Sometimes we stood barefoot up there and jumped off. We even sat on the very top. Jumped off from that too. We touched the keys without washing our hands first, smearing margarine, jam, chocolate, ice cream, and mud across everything. We napped facedown on the ivories, drooling onto the keys. Licked them too. We beat them with things other than our fingers—recorders, pencils, rulers, our doll Rika's hands, even though her fingers were fused together. Instead of pushing down on the keys with our fingers, we used our nails to raise them, trying to pry them loose. We didn't ease the lid down, we slammed it. Sometimes we lowered it partway and let gravity do the rest. Either method always set the strings trembling, and we could hear their muffled cries inside the piano. We sat on the bench and put our feet to the lid, pushing until the bench teetered on only two legs. We balanced there, rocking, reading manga. We hadn't learned how to use the pedals yet, but we stomped on them. Sometimes while I was playing, my sister would dive under the keys and push the pedals with her hands or her rear.

Mom would scold and yell and say things like, "Don't you feel sorry for Mr. Piano?" but she was another bad guy. She never separated us from the piano. She was equally guilty.

I imagine this kind of piano abuse happened in a lot of households. And me and my sister think it's not at all unnatural that the pianos vowed to retaliate with an uprising.

ONCE THE PIANOS LEARNED TO BITE, the ones who got the short end of the stick were people like, for example, my piano teacher. People who really love music.

Mom didn't send us to some corporate music school like the one she went to. She relied on her friends' connections to find a teacher who was giving private lessons out of her home. Mom found a lady who had won several national piano competitions in her teens and studied abroad in the Czech Republic. Our teacher still appeared in concerts from time to time and had a banker husband who loved classical music.

Once a week, Mom packed us into her car and took us to our lessons. Our teacher's home was an apartment just as tiny as ours, and one room was almost entirely occupied by a single grand piano. I have no idea how they got that piano inside that room, but unlike our upright, that grand was cherished. Our teacher had a son, a boy right between me and my sister's ages. That was T. Of course he had a real name, but in the end he was a T, so I think that's good enough.

T was an amazing piano player—of course, so were all the other Ts in the world. After all, T had been listening to his mother play since the moment he was born, and she never stopped teaching him. If he wasn't at school or eating, and she wasn't with another student, she was making him practice, so obviously he was amazing. While I was sick of doing Czerny over and over, he'd already mastered all of Bach's Inventions and was about halfway through the Sinfonias, and while the faces I pulled as I played my way through Bartok's bizarre music had my sister in stitches, he was crushing Chopin and Mozart's sonatas. T was entering junior competitions even before me and my sister started lessons with his mother, and he'd won some prizes too. There were even newspaper articles about him, each of them framed and sitting on a knickknack shelf over their toilet.

While me and my sister had our lessons, Mom sat silently in the corner on a chair, making sure we didn't get up to any trouble. In the car on the ride home, she compared both of us to T nonstop.

"You should be as serious as T!" she warned. Sometimes her coaxing was sweeter: "If you would just practice enough, I'm sure you'd be able to play as well as him."

Me and my sister both knew that no matter how serious we got, no matter how much we practiced, there was no way that was going to happen. It was baffling how our mother couldn't see that.

Once in elementary school, I wrote an essay about how I wanted to become a manga artist when I grew up, and when I got home, my mother, fed up, said, "Don't you mean a pianist?" Shortly after that, my little sister wrote in an essay that she wanted to run a clothing store, which made Mom exclaim, "I can't believe you two!"

T wrote, "I want to be a piano when I grow up." His mom told our mom about that, laughing as she said, "I don't know what to do with him." Mom in turn used this as an example—"That's how much T loves the piano." I don't know what kind of message that was supposed to send us.

Even T's weird little habit was a virtue as far as Mom was concerned. You see, little by little, T started dozing off as he played.

We saw this more than once when Mom brought us to our teacher's apartment for lessons. T had to practice until his mother's students arrived, and on days when we got there a little early, we could watch him.

At first we thought his eyes were closed because he was entranced by the beauty of the music he was playing. His performance continued without a hitch, so that's what we assumed. Even his mother thought that. My sister decided that if she copied him, she might look like she was better at the piano too. But when she tried, her arms went all over the place and her already terrible performance got even worse.

Eventually T's head began lolling back and forth, and it was clear to anyone watching that he was asleep. But even then, there were no mistakes in his performance. His fingers pressed the correct keys with unbelievable speed, and he decrescendoed and crescendoed with feeling, following the score exactly.

His mother worried about this a lot, and we heard that she scolded him all the time.

When we arrived at our teacher's apartment, we would hear T playing. Even as our teacher beckoned us in, the sound of him in the piano room continued. When she let us into the room, we saw T's closed eyes were red and swollen with tears, and his head jerked with his magnificent performance, like he was playing to the peanut gallery. Since we were there, our teacher was smiling, but it was clear that she was upset.

Our mom, however, was really and truly moved. "Now look there. T is practicing himself to sleep!" she said.

Eventually, T fell asleep during a recital. It was the only recital our teacher ever had us give in the three years we took lessons from her.

Me and my sister weren't doing a four-handed piece, but Mom still made us wear matching white dresses. And of course, around our waists were a blue ribbon for me and a pink one for my sister. The dresses weren't as poofy as I'd wanted, and the ribbons weren't nearly as pastel as I'd imagined them—they were pretty eye-scorching shades of blue and pink.

T walked on stage, bowed, and sat at the bench, but the moment he placed his hands over the keys, his head snapped back so hard I almost jumped. There was such force I almost thought his head would fall off, roll across the stage, and plop right into my lap in the first row. Head flopping the whole time, T played Liszt's *Liebesträume* to the very end. His performance was magnificent. I don't think there was a single flub. The moment the song ended, T opened his eyes, stood and bowed, fighting a yawn.

Mom didn't hesitate to give him wild applause. Up until she started, no one had clapped. Carried along by our mother, the concert hall drowned in the sound of applause. As I clapped, I glanced over my shoulder to peek at our teacher. Her face was bone white, and one of her eyes was twitching. "Hey, keep your eyes on the stage," said my mother, yanking my sleeve. Then she leaned down close to my ear and whispered, "Come on, when you get as good as T, you'll be able to play it like that in your sleep, too." Even having watched that entire display, Mom was truly moved.

Of course she doesn't say that kind of thing anymore.

Now, tears in her eyes, she says, "I'm so glad you two didn't turn out like T. Just stay my sweet little girls."

Of course now my sister and I love the piano like we never did before. We treat it much better.

"Pianos don't have a brain, right? That's why they're so stupid," my sister says as she strokes the wood.

"That's right," I agree. After all, when the pianos revolted, they left us alone. In fact we were overjoyed. Because we didn't have to practice piano anymore.

Me and my sister do have brains, so we come up with new and more effective ways for the pianos to exact their revenge against humanity.

"If I were a piano, I'd fall on top of you. Bam! And then I would crush you," I suggest, turning toward my sister. She shrieks with laughter.

"You won't do that, right?" She climbs on top of the bench, spreads her arms wide, and hugs the piano. Then she rubs her cheek against the top. "You're a good piano. You won't do awful things like my big sister."

"Well, what would you do then, if you were a piano?" I ask as I open the lid a crack. My sister thinks.

"Hmm . . . Push and crush! I'd push you and crush you!"

"Oh come on, you're just copying me."

"Am not! You said you were going to fall on me. I could dodge that. See, what I would do is, if I were a piano, I'd aim right for you and fly—*pyoon!*—and then on the other side of you, there'd be a wall, and I'd squish you between the wall and me. Squish you flat."

"That's basically the same," I sigh. I feel bad that my little sister is so stupid. But I feel even worse for our piano.

"Hey, did you hear that?" I ask it. "You could have done something like that. We would have run away though, me and my sister. But you could have done that."

I plop both my hands on the piano.

When I do, the piano *bites my fingers*. I say bites, but it doesn't really hurt or anything. The right black or white keys grab the right fingers, sink until they meet the bottom of the keyboard, and then pass those fingers off to the next keys.

The song begins. I'm pretty sure it's one of Bach's Sinfonias. I don't know which number or what key, though it's definitely minor. I heard T play it once.

My sister leaps off the piano bench, so I can sit down. I look like I'm giving a brilliant piano performance all while standing, but I haven't done anything. I'm just giving my body over. The piano itself is biting my fingers and through them temporarily taking control of the muscles of my arms all the way up to my shoulders, using my body to perform the music. Standing doesn't mess up anything, but still I sit on the bench. My sister crawls under the keyboard beneath the highest notes, wrapping her arms around her knees and sitting quietly.

This is why we don't have to practice anymore. It's the same when my sister puts her hands on the keys. The same for Mom, for anybody.

All of a sudden the pianos were alive, so they didn't need skilled players anymore. Now the pianos borrow people's hands and play whatever they like however they like. If they don't have a person's hands, they're as silent as they ever were.

When this first happened, a lot of people said pianos weren't alive. Nobody could believe it. I saw some scientist on TV saying, "No. Pianos are not living beings. They have no *metabolism*." "Metabolism" appeared in big letters at the bottom of the screen. But after a while, sure enough, they were saying, "I'm sorry. I was wrong. They *are* alive." This is because pianos that had been neglected long enough or whose owners ignored them because they thought they were creepy started dying.

Pianos who were opened daily, given hands on their keys, and allowed to bite those hands and play, didn't die. If you need a metabolism to be alive, I think a piano's metabolism must be performing music.

It's easy to tell when a piano is dead, just like with any other organism. When a piano breathes its last, its wood goes limp and it can't keep its piano shape anymore, collapsing into a sloppy mess on the floor. If you just leave it there, it'll start to stink and maggots will appear, and if you leave it even longer, it'll turn into this watery goop, sinking into the flooring or carpet and rotting the foundations of the house. If it gets that far along, you're really in trouble. You won't be able to clean it up—all you can do is renovate.

Of course the thing that actually convinced people was the emergence of all the Ts. Because of them, nobody could say pianos weren't alive anymore.

When I say Ts, I mean kids like our teacher's. Kids who liked piano and were really good at it and could make pianos react like they were almost alive just by touching them with their miraculous fingertips, the few kids who, once the pianos were on the brink of coming alive and only needed the slightest encouragement to explode into the next step of their evolution, transformed into pianos themselves.

We only found out later, but T's ability to keep playing piano so well in his sleep was a sign. In order to give the piano the kick it needed, T had to use so much of his own strength, and of course that put him to sleep.

Naturally, nowadays the pianos give the best performances even if the players are asleep. The story is that T and kids like him metamorphosed, pulled along by the final wave of evolution that allowed the pianos to come alive, and since all the pianos in the world are now fully living beings, there won't be another T. That's what they said on this TV show, "In Search of the Mystery behind the Transformers: Piano Phenomenon." Come to think of it, on the day of our final piano lesson, wasn't T crawling around on his hands and knees? That was the last time I saw him in his human form.

That day when the lesson was done and we left the room, T was down on all fours in the entryway, his backside to us. Our teacher growled out, "What exactly do you think you're doing?" but T didn't start, didn't even move. "You're blocking the entryway," she said, her voice even more terrifying, but still he didn't move. I had never seen T mess around like that before, so I got a little excited, and before I knew it, I had put my hands on his back and vaulted right over him. My sister shrieked with glee and copied me. T's back was strangely solid. And it felt too flat somehow. Like a wooden board. But other than that, his back was warm. Like a normal person's. I think that's the only time I ever touched him when he was in human form. T remained on all fours, even as my sister and me put on our shoes, and when we waved goodbye to him, he just raised his head to say goodbye in return. The next week, our teacher called to say T wasn't feeling well, so our lessons were canceled. The same call came the next week, and the next, on and on. Somewhere in there, pianos all over the world came to life and raised a big stink.

According to "In Search of the Mystery behind the Transformers: Piano Phenomenon," the transformation of T and others like him happened like this. At first they crawled all over the place, but later they stopped moving, no matter what. By then, the skin's lignification had already begun. The skin got darker too. As their bodies began to expand, their human features started to disappear, until they assumed the form of an upright or a grand piano. The form is apparently based on the type of piano they played most often as a human. The entire transformation took about a month.

Mom started crying and couldn't finish watching the episode. Me and my sister got bored after they finished showing the CG video of the transformation process, so we ran off to the tatami room to give some attention to our piano.

We heard Mom say to Dad, "I feel bad for T. Really. His mother, too. I suppose it's just bad luck."

I feel the same. I don't know if I feel bad for T, but I do feel bad for his mom.

That's why me and my sister haven't stopped going to her place once a week.

ONCE WE ARRIVE AT OUR teacher's apartment, we hop, skip, and jump our way across the parking lot out front, heading for a feral, weather-beaten grand piano. My sister throws open the lid with a bang and begins playing Chopin's *Revolutionary*. Of course it's the piano doing the playing. The feral piano's lid has been left open, so it sounds pretty bad. But when *Revolutionary* plays on a piano so out of tune, it actually sounds kind of amazing.

I wrap my arms around the prop holding the piano's lid open and peek inside. The hammers connected to the keys that grab my sister's fingers pound away at the strings, and the sound swells along the strange curve of the piano, stealing up over my face and filling the air. Maybe pianos were alive from the start—way, way back, even before they became like this. Happy, I place both my hands on the grand's flanks and

jump up, putting my weight on it like I'm mounting a gymnastics bar.

We see a lot of feral pianos around, illegally dumped by people who are afraid a piano will die in their house. The ferals abandoned along school routes tend to keep on living. Kids can't leave feral cats alone, let alone feral pianos.

This particular grand piano is the one my sister and I played at our lessons. The transformed T has become the magnificent grand piano in his mother's home, but that means there isn't room for this one, so it was tossed out. Luckily, there are a lot of kids in this apartment complex, and more elementary and middle schoolers in the neighborhood, so it hasn't been too hard for this piano to keep on living.

When *Revolutionary* finishes, Mom calls for us. We take the elevator to our teacher's floor and press the intercom button. She emerges to let us in. She's looking older lately. Even though she and Mom are about the same age.

Me and my sister run straight to the room where we used to have our lessons, the room that's now T's.

I think our mom and our teacher are friends now. They have tea in the living room and talk about stuff.

I think me and my sister are friends with T, too. Even though back when he was just our teacher's son, we barely said hello when we found him dashing off a disgustingly perfect performance.

Carefully I place my hands on T's lid and heave it open. This is his back. My sister lifts the prop, and I set the lid in place. T's huge beautiful innards glisten below me. He's completely different from the feral piano downstairs. Not a speck of rust on his strings, tuning pins glittering.

My sister lifts the keyboard lid and removes the felt cover, red as a tongue, and the blinding white keys appear. I remember T had such strong perfect teeth back when he was a human.

She pulls out the bench. I sit and set my hands on the keys. Soft and round like I'm holding eggs in my palms, just like our teacher taught us.

T, who was once our teacher's son, bites my fingers. I don't really understand how, but it feels like instead of the skin of my fingertips, T is tugging at the thin, thin strings of nerves and muscles beneath.

"Hey, play a song I know, T," I tell him, cutting in before he can start his performance. I feel him waver for just a moment. Yes, he definitely hesitated. I think he was rethinking his song choice. For me.

He begins his performance.

"Oh, I know this one, I know it!" I shout.

"I know it!" my sister shouts. Tchaikovsky's "Dance of the Sugar Plum Fairy" from *The Nutcracker*. My sister begins to spin and spin. She's trying to dance along.

I butt in. "That's not how the dance goes."

"Then how does it go?"

I have no idea. But it's not that.

When she realizes I don't know the answer, she grins and tries to raise one leg, but it hits the wall first. She doesn't seem to mind though, raising both hands and joining her palms above her head, wriggling her whole body. "Dance of the Sugar Plum Fairy" ends. When I don't take my hands off the keyboard, "Waltz of the Flowers" begins.

I let T do as he will, taking in the strike of the hammers and the quivering of the strings with only the barest touch of my fingers.

Of course I can hear the song with my ears. And I understand that what I'm hearing is beautiful. But I don't taste the kind of pleasure I felt back when it was me and my sister in our tatami room, me calmly playing as I ignored her screams and rants. Back then, me and the sound were under only my body's orders. My body was the music itself. It's different now. That kind of feeling will never happen again. Me and the sound, we're under the piano's orders. My body is just a part of the instrument. The one tasting that pleasure is T. He's playing and ignoring the world, just the way I ignored my sister.

Of course, none of this bothers me at all.

One way or another, humanity has lost the right to play the piano under their own power, but that's nothing to people like me and my sister. I really do feel bad for our teacher, though. She has all this talent she worked so hard to polish, but she can't use it to give any performances, plus her son's like this.

Right now, me and my sister are obsessed with T and the other pianos, but sooner or later, we'll get tired of them. We'll stop coming by. Friendships change with the passing of time, that's just the way it is. Our mom will probably do something about our upright eventually. Ask the ward office how to get rid of it or call someone to euthanize it. People doing that kind of work have popped up recently. We've seen flyers in our mailbox.

I'm fine with that. My sister will be too, of course. Mom might cry a little, but she'll probably be fine. 🐵

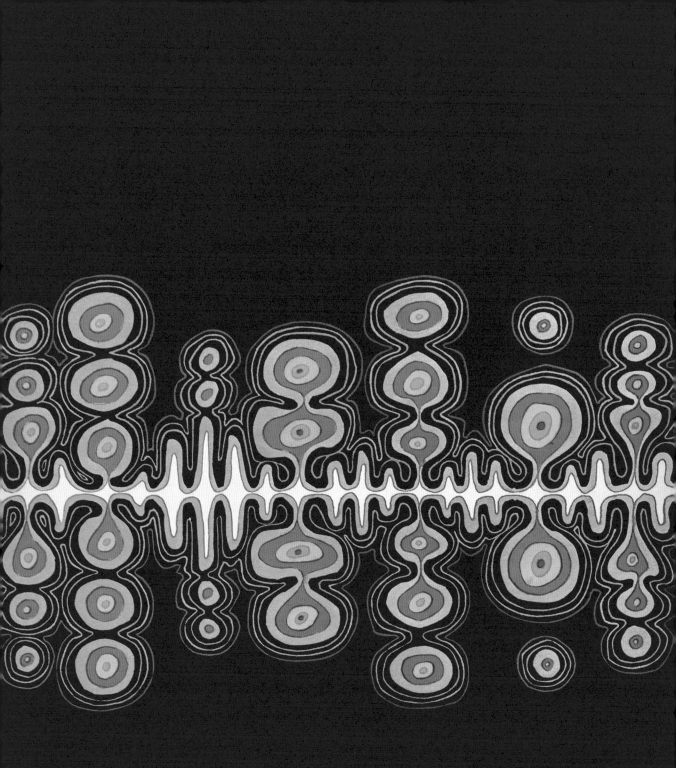

Michel Otthoffer

Ichiyō Higuchi

———

The Music of the Koto

translated by Hitomi Yoshio

I.

THE SUN AND THE MOON illuminate the sky and all that abide below. In spring, the flowers bloom for everyone to enjoy. Why is it, then, that the storm brings so much turmoil on this lone treetop? Here was a child, innocent and alone, dragged through misfortune as his family was scattered like leaves and broken branches. For fourteen years, he'd been pelted by the rain and battered by the wind—in spring, in autumn. He was adrift in this cruel and uncertain world.

His mother had left when he was just four years old. She had no wish to abandon her child to escape her own suffering, but her parents, seeing the decline in the fortunes of her husband's family, reasoned with her and begged her to return to them. "If you entrust your life to an unworthy man, you'll only waste away your life in tears. As hard as it is to leave a child behind, at least there is only one…" These words made their way into her still youthful ears and took hold of her heart. She was not sorry to leave the child's father. But her beloved boy… What would happen to him after she left? The thought was so agonizing she could have coughed blood. But the duty she felt toward her parents held her in an iron grip, and in the end, her heart was too weak to resist. And so, knowing that their life was about to collapse like pillars of frost, she left her home and her child—and the father of her child.

After she left, the child's father would come to her parents' house to seek her out. Sometimes he would be alone, sometimes he would bring the boy. He would even try to leave the boy at their doorstep. "I don't care what becomes of me," he begged and pleaded. "But please, come back, for the boy and his future. I won't say forever…just give him five more years, until he can take care of himself." He grasped at the hope that she would return—after all, what mother can resist doting on her child? Surely she would find it unbearable to remain apart. So when would she come back? On the fifteenth, or perhaps on the twentieth? Perhaps any day now—today or tomorrow. He waited and waited, but the days passed in vain. On his final visit, she was nowhere to be found. What had become of her? Was she a wet nurse now, looking after another family's children? Had she become the wife of another man? Their vows of one hundred years proved to be empty.

Half a year passed. The boy's father was no longer what he used to be. The townspeople praised the boy's mother for being wise enough to leave him. Only a few felt sorry for the father and boy who had been left behind. Who could blame them? The father was now a drunk. He drank to forget his pain, drank away the sorrow that shadowed his heart. The more he drank, the more depressed and dejected he became. Who would sympathize with such a selfish and stubborn man? By the end of the year, the father and son had nothing to keep them warm, let alone a roof to protect them from the rain and the dew. Still, the child had only his father to rely upon. He looked up to him as if taking shelter under a large tree. Though their futon were thin in the cheap lodgings where they sheltered for the night, the boy still took comfort in his father's presence.

But this did not last long. Before the boy was ten, his father met a bitter end. He had joined a celebration at a wealthy house that had opened its doors to everyone in the village. Sake flowed freely from the barrels, and he drank to his heart's content. "How heavenly this sake is! Drinking this will surely guide me to paradise," he told himself as he drank cup after cup on an empty stomach. On his way home, he collapsed beneath a pine tree and died.

Now the boy was truly alone. No one lent him a hand or offered to take care of him. The boy had no hope for his future, no desire to live a decent life. At first, he was envious of those who were blessed with fathers and mothers. He remembered that he, too, had a mother once. I wonder where she is and what she's doing? he thought to himself. He longed to be with her again. But thinking about how she had abandoned him, and how his father fell apart and ended up dead, the boy began to hate his mother as if she were the devil itself.

The boy used to weep when people asked him about his father, and where his mother had gone. But no more. Once he had concluded that there was no compassion in this world, he felt that even those who took pity on him were insincere and were laughing at

him behind his back. "To hell with all this," he swore with a twisted heart. "If this misery is life, let it be miserable till the end. Let's see how low my life will fall." Even the gods and buddhas were his enemy now. Who could he have appealed to? His pitiful circumstance drove him to think extreme thoughts.

Looking out from behind his wildly disheveled hair, the boy's eyes gleamed as if ready to pierce whatever they landed on. His face was covered with grime—of the pleasing features his face once had, no trace remained. "Beware of that brat. He's not to be trusted. Don't let your guard down." People pointed at him and talked about him openly, and even the police considered him a criminal. At festivals and fairs where crowds gathered, accusations of "Pickpocket! Thief!" were flung at him. How he hated them all.

People are blind and believe what others say. The rumors spread far and wide, and once spread, they were impossible to dispel. Kingo Watanabe became known as a true criminal, even though he had done nothing. Before long, people shuddered at his name and called him the Great Criminal of Meiji. As for the boy himself, sometimes he wanted to run away to a distant land, and sometimes he thought about ending it all. Unable to cope with the injustice, he stood on the riverbank time and again, looking out over the water as if for the last time. But it was easier said than done. How could he end his own life?

Though he had no care for his life, he still needed to eat and sleep. During the day, he wandered about aimlessly and found work when he needed. At night, he would sleep wherever he could find a place to rest and dream. And so he drifted from day to day. Time passed, and as he grew, so did his twisted heart.

II.

IT WAS THE RICE HARVEST SEASON in Negishi, where the melancholy winds blew over the sacred pine of Ogyō. A woman named Shizu Morie lived in a house with only her maids as companions. One day the servants noticed a beggar boy hanging around the house. They whispered and gossiped, uneasy about his behavior. But in truth, there was no need to worry about locking the gates. Even the persimmon tree, which was heavily laden with fruit, was left alone. One month passed without incident, and they forgot about the boy. Then, at some point, strange sounds began to reach the mistress's sensitive ears.

One gloomy evening, as the autumn rain fell steadily, she sat playing her beloved koto by the lamplight. The music had a beautiful melancholy to it. She heard the temple bells ringing in the Ueno forest. It must be late, she thought, and put her music aside to listen more closely. Just then, amidst the sound of rain dripping from the eaves and the autumn wind whistling through the treetops, she heard a rustling outside. She didn't know what it was, but she kept hearing it night after night.

From beneath the eaves, she could see the tall pine tree in the distance. If she had been asked why she lived alone, she would have answered that it was because of her music. For many years she had devoted herself to the gentle music of the koto, pouring all she had into it. Shizu was nineteen years old. She was thin and frail like a willow branch that sways in the wind, but when she sat in front of the koto with her pick, she played with such intensity and composure that— *Scattering from the world the dust of worries and troubles, like the pine breeze that weaves through the branches of a willow tree, the mountain goddess descends and guides her hand over the strings. Dream or reality, the music is ushered in.* With a smile on her lips, she would play her music, blissfully oblivious to the wind and rain, the roaring thunder.

It was the tenth month. The first frost had fallen, and the moon shone over the red autumn leaves. Who had polished the moon to shine so brightly? The colors appeared as bold as rouge on an old woman's face. The moon, shining in the cloudless sky, illuminated everything, from the lofty buildings and towers to the dog's bed between the boards of the shack; the pond of an old house where a woman lived, hidden away and abandoned, where only the frost shone bright over the withered reeds; the lonely sound of water dripping in the garden of the mountain hermitage; the scarecrow in a rice field, and the trickle of a small stream. Even the legendary shores of Suma, Akashi, and Matsushima, famous for their beauty in the moonlight, were enveloped into one. The pure appeared pure,

the muddy appeared muddy. The moon shone in perfect serenity, illuminating everything equally. On such a night, the clear music of the koto would rise to the heavens, as far as it could go. Beautiful and charming, pure and exquisite, just like the music of the heavens.

On this very night, Shizu's koto music awakened a soul in this miserable world. For fourteen years, this boy had been pelted by rain, and his twisted heart had grown so hard, not even an arrow could penetrate it. He had been destined to follow the dreadful fate of his father, whose corpse was left in the fields to rot. Or perhaps his notoriety would catch up to him, and he'd waste away his life in prison, in chains.

But on this night, the tenderness that lurked deep in the boy's heart was awakened by the harmony of the koto music under the moonlight. The tears that touched his cheeks for the first time—were they dewdrops? They were more precious to him than the grandest castles.

Was he moved on this night by love or affection? He had no idea what the koto player even looked like. Her voice could only be heard faintly over the wooden fence, but she had made him happy—she had also made him feel ashamed. Suddenly, Kingo felt a strong yearning for his mother, whom he had resented like the devil itself. He realized that this world was too precious to give up. The moon was even brighter now. The fragrance of the chrysanthemums that bloomed on the fence filled his sleeves, filled his heart. The night wind dispersed the clouds that had covered his mind, as the music of the koto filled the air. The music would be his friend for a hundred years, filling his heart with yearning for a hundred more. He would step into the world where one hundred flowers bloom in profusion. 🐒

Note from the translator: This story was originally published in 1893, just two months after Ichiyō moved to Ryūsenji-cho in Tokyo and opened a shop to support her family. The title, "The Music of the Koto" (*Koto no ne*), is a reference to a poem in the Suma chapter of *The Tale of Genji,* and there are allusions to classical poetry throughout the story. During the Meiji period, a woman rarely left her husband unless her family, often of a higher standing, intervened. In such cases, the woman did not usually get custody of the children, especially if they were male, who remained part of the father's household. This dilemma of a married woman facing the decision to suffer in her marriage or get a divorce and leave her child behind is explored from the woman's point of view in "The Thirteenth Night" (Jūsan'ya, 1895).

This story was previously translated as "The Sound of the Koto" by Robert Lyons Danley in his book *In the Shade of Spring Leaves* (New York: Norton, 1981).

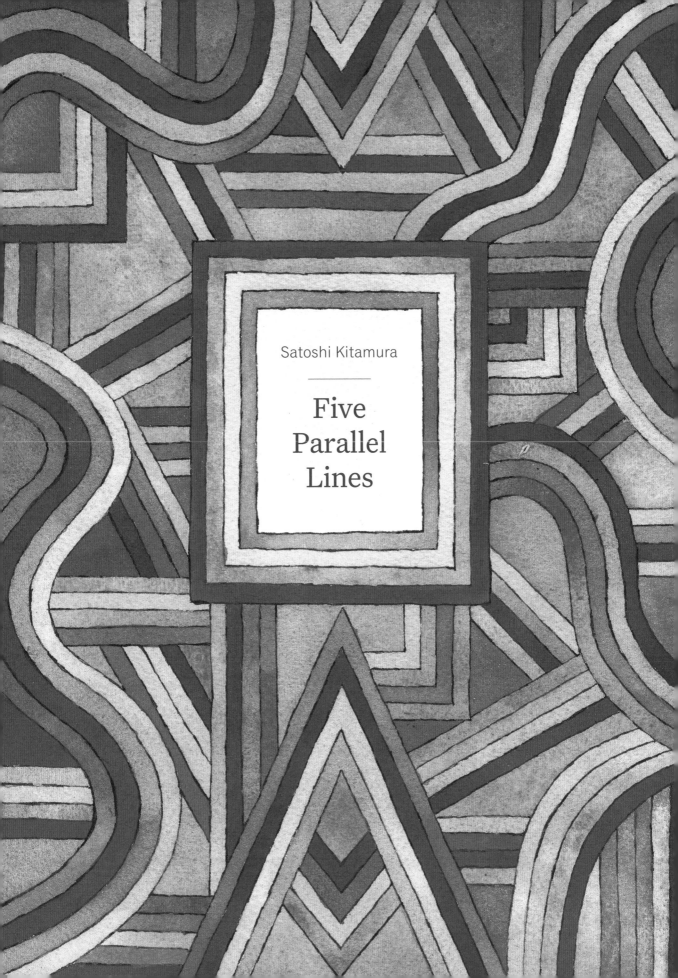

The Man on the Piano

The pianist walked onto the stage. He lay down on top of the piano. Soon he was fast asleep and began to snore. That made the audience sleepy. They all fell asleep and snored. It was meant to be a solo piano piece but turned out to be a symphony. Although no one was awake to listen to it. When the audience woke up the pianist had already left the stage.

The Giraffe

Maestro was practicing his violin in his second-floor apartment when he felt
someone's eyes on him. Turning round, he saw a giraffe in the window.
It was grinning, as if to say, "Maybe you are not as good as you think you are."
Since then, every time Maestro plays a concert, he keeps seeing the giraffe
somewhere in the auditorium. It always has that same grin.

Cul-de-Sax

In the late 1940s, Lester Young once turned up at a gig with a new saxophone. When he began to play, the audience became quite puzzled because all they could hear was a piano trio, and not a single note from Lester's horn. Someone noticed that his tenor sax had no tone holes or bell opening. It was a blind metal tube in the shape of a saxophone. But Lester "played" as if nothing was amiss. The way he tilted his instrument and his faint smile around the mouthpiece were the same as usual. He looked at ease and content. Then the audience started to feel that they were hearing his sax after all. Yes, it was Lester Young's horn wailing, if a little silently.

A Walk

A pianist took his piano for a walk one afternoon. It was thrilled to be out in the sun for the first time in months. In the park the piano was off leash and ran around singing a divertimento to itself. When the pianist stopped at a cafe for coffee, the piano quietly sat outside waiting for its master. But on the way home they met another pianist and her piano, and the two pianos became so excited that they couldn't stop barking a rhapsody at each other. The two pianists had a hard time separating them. When they got home, the piano calmed down and softly hummed a polonaise.

Non-Euclidean

One day Ludwig van Beethoven and Carl Friedrich Gauss bumped into each other at a cafe. Gauss sat next to Beethoven, looked round, and then whispered in the composer's ear. "Ludwig, I'll tell you a secret." The mathematician looked into Beethoven's eyes. "If you have parallel lines on an elliptical sphere, they never stay parallel. They eventually meet . . . Do you get it, Ludwig?"

Beethoven thought for quite a while before replying: "Does it mean that all those notes I write on the score eventually merge? My symphony ends up reduced to a single note. Is that what you're saying, Carl Friedrich?"

"I'm afraid so," answered Gauss.

"Oh, mein Gott!" muttered Beethoven.

"But, Ludwig," Gauss said, "don't tell anyone."

Hamed Rajabpour and Nariman Ghorbani

Taruho Inagaki

———

Eleven One-Second Stories

translated by Jeffrey Angles

INTRODUCTION

CONTEMPORARY LITERARY HISTORIANS frequently remember the prolific writer Taruho Inagaki (1900–1977) as one of the grand innovators of Japanese modernist literature. Indeed, one of his admirers and friends, the prominent novelist Yukio Mishima (1925–1970), wrote in the book *On Authors* (*Sakkaron*) that in the literature of the Shōwa period (1926–1989), Taruho was a rare genius who held a place equivalent to the astronauts in history; literary history could be divided "into the world before Taruho and the world after Taruho." This high appraisal stems from several factors—namely, Taruho's wild experiments in forging a new Japanese modernist style, his highly sensitive and introspective nature, and his extremely imaginative, loosely associative style of writing, which blurs the boundaries between reality and fantasy, fiction and nonfiction, poetry and prose, and adult and children's literature.

One Thousand One-Second Stories (1923) is a classic of Japanese experimental fiction. With their surreal plots and playful avoidance of standard punctuation and spacing, the following stories from that collection may seem to be little more than amusing, quirky, almost childlike monkey business, but literary historian Myriam Sas has argued that this work represents an evocation of a particular vision of modernity: a futuristic world dominated by "a poetry of rhythms and displacements, flickers and exchanges." The stories depict "a universe of accretions, where narrative proceeds by metonymy and leaps rather than by the proceedings of causal logic."[1] Unlike many of his contemporaries who believed that the increasing speed of modern life had dulled people's perception, Taruho showed in these stories that modern life provided numerous opportunities for poignant aesthetic experiences, and much of his early writing celebrates small, random encounters with the "new" that might momentarily liberate a viewer from the constraints of mundane reality.

———

1. Miryam Sas, "Subject, City, Machine," in *Histories of the Future,* edited by Daniel Rosenberg and Susan Harding (Durham, NC: Duke University Press, 2005), 217.

THE MAN IN THE MOON

I was listening to the strains of a guitar leaking through
a yellow window in a painting of a night landscape
when I heard a spring pop loose in a clock   and a
huge mechanized diorama of Mr. Moon began to rise
in the distance

  It stopped about one meter above the ground   and
a man wearing an opera hat   jumped nimbly
down   *Whoa!* As I was watching   he lit a cigarette
and started down the tree-lined street   I followed
The trees cast such interesting silhouettes   that all
of my attention was taken up by the shadows
when I realized the man walking right of me had
vanished   I pricked up my ears   but I didn't hear
anything remotely resembling the sound of footsteps
I came back to the place where I had started   and
discovered that the moon had at some point risen
high in the sky   and the pinwheels were whirring as
they spun in the quiet nighttime breeze

EAVESDROPPING IN THE SHADOWS OF A WAREHOUSE ONE NIGHT

"Mr. Moon's out tonight"
"That guy's made of tin"
"What?   Made of tin you say?"
"Well mister   I guarantee he's nickel-plated at the
very least"
(That was all I overheard)

UNE MÉMOIRE

A gentle spring moon was hanging in the middle of the sky   The forests and hills and rivers were misty and blue   and off in the distance the backbone of a rocky mountain glittered faintly

The moonlight rained silently down upon the entire scene   From far off in the distance came the sounds of a flute   *Toodle-toodle-loo*   It seemed so forlorn   so filled with nostalgia   The sound was so faint   that it was hard to know if one was really hearing it or not   I pricked up my ears   It seemed someone was singing   The voice seemed full of blame   full of grief   but I had no idea what it was saying

Toodle-toodle-loo…loo…

The notes of the flute   made the moonlight come raining down all the more

And then   from somewhere I heard a voice whisper   "It was probably   on a night like this…"

Surprised I asked back   "Huh?   What are you talking about?"

But there was no response   For a while the moonlight simply continued to rain down   as if nothing had happened

But then   I heard the whisper again   coming from nowhere in particular   This time it sounded a little peeved   as if it were giving up   as if it were sad

"It was probably   on a night like this…"

Flustered   I piped up again   "Huh? What's that?"

But the voice made no attempt to answer

Silence

I noticed a rock by my shoe and picked it up but before I could hurl it into the distance   I let it fall from my hand   as if I were overcome with disappointment

Under the blue moonlit sky   the mountains hills and forests were as misty as a dream

Toodle-toodle-loo…loo…

UN ÉNIGME

—*onamoonliteveningabutterflyturnedintoadragonfly*
—Huh?
—*didthedragonflyblowitsnose?*
—What's that again?
—*didyoucatchafishintissuepaper?*
—What? What're you saying?
—*thereisvalueinnotunderstanding*

A PUZZLE

—ツキヨノバンニチョウチョウガトンボニナッタ
—え？
—トンボノハナカンダカイ
—なんだって？
—ハナカミデサカナヲツッタカイ
—なに　なんだって？
—ワカラナイノガネウチダトサ

THE TIME THE MIST GOT THE BETTER OF ME

It was near midnight and a white mist had settled
over everything   when I passed beneath the eye
of a gas lamp and entered an alley   only to find a wide
asphalt road there   There were show windows on
both sides and in them were electric and gas lamps
lit up as bright as day   The beautiful hats and clothing
were dazzling but there wasn't a single person to
be seen anywhere   Even so I could hear the *screech*
of the glass doors opening and closing   and the
murmuring of people crowded together   As I was
passing by I peeked in one of the larger stores   Several
things that looked like shimmering heat waves
were busily jostling about   on the staircase at the
back   The sight creeped me out and so I ran for all
I was worth for two or three blocks   Or at least
that's what I thought   At some point I had left the
alley   and I was standing in front of a deserted stone
staircase that led up to a dark but familiar-looking
house   At the top of the stars I watched as the electric
light quivered . . .

THE POCKETED MOON

One evening   Mr. Moon put himself in his pocket
and went out for a stroll   He was on a sloping street
when his shoelace came untied   He was bending
over to tie it when Mr. Moon rolled out of his
pocket   and started rolling down the asphalt which
was still wet from an earlier drizzle   He rolled and
rolled and rolled and rolled until it looked like he
would never stop   Mr. Moon chased after him   but
Mr. Moon picked up speed as he rolled away   so the
distance between Mr. Moon and Mr. Moon gradually
grew   And that is how Mr. Moon lost sight of himself
in the bluish mist so far below

MOONLIGHT MOONSHINERS

One night   not long before dawn   I heard some
voices on the balcony   I peeked through the
keyhole   and saw two or three dark shadows
turning some sort of machine   Earlier I had noticed
an article in the newspaper about a gang who
snuck onto people's balconies   in the middle of the
night when the moon was high   and used a secret
contraption recently invented in London   to make
moonshine out of moonlight   I put my automatic
pistol against the keyhole and shot   *POW, POW,
POW, POW, POW...*   The bullets struck the roofs
and the road below the balcony and I heard the
sound of breaking glass

I opened the door thinking I would jump out
onto the balcony   when something rushed in like
a gust of wind beside me   It blew me off my feet
When I regained my composure and went onto the
balcony   there was no one there   A single bottle
was perched at the edge of the roof   so I picked it up
and held it to the light   There was something that
looked like water inside   I tried shaking it and the
cork popped off all on its own   *POP!*   The sound
resonated through the still night air   A great deal of
vapor rose from the mouth of the bottle   and right
before my eyes it melted away to become part of the
moonlight . . .

I kept watching until everything in the bottle was
gone   And that was all   other than the fact that the
moon seemed a bit paler than usual

L'INCIDENT AU CONCERT

The orchestra had no sooner started playing *The North
Star Fantasy*   than a puff of yellow smoke rose
from the musicians   and spread throughout the
concert hall

The workers by the entrance panicked and opened
every window they could   trying to get all the
smoke out   When it was gone   the orchestra   and
the spectators were all gone as well   The only
thing in the huge hall was a dazzling shower of light
from the gas lamps

What on earth had happened?   Everyone in
the hall had disappeared   so there was no way to
know   but the public arrived at the theory that
probably   this mystery   was the result of the sky
being so crammed full of falling stardust that evening

TOUR DU CHAT-NOIR

As the moon rose   I was walking around a dark
cone-shaped tower that was standing there   when
I heard a sound   *Snap!*   I fell into pitch blackness
But no   I was inside the tower   The floor and
walls were decorated with the same odd geometric
patterns   and a black cat was seated on the round
table in the middle   I tried to pet it   but I heard
the sound of a switch and the tower began to rotate
around and around   It was growing gradually
narrower   I was caught up in a whirl of red and
yellow and tossed up into the peak of the cone
Bam!   I was thrown outside   I did two or three
somersaults in the air   and got caught on an
electrical wire   but the wire broke and I fell onto
a horse cart passing below

   The driver who was nodding off at the reins didn't
notice   I lay unconscious on the straw as the cart
carried me   over the bluish moonlit road   toward
the distant countryside

STAR OR FIRECRACKER?

One evening   I was singing *Rule Britannia* when I
tossed my cap into the air   and it hit the stars   One
star came falling down   making a *clink* on the brick
road   I picked up the white thing lying there and
went over to a gas lamp   I was taking a good look at
it thinking that I might make it into a medallion
when *crack!* It broke apart

   I ran to the police booth on the opposite corner
   "You probably picked up a firecracker by mistake
Over there is where the real stars fall"   he said as he
led me to the scene
   He took out his flashlight   but there was nothing
to see
   "I guess maybe it was a star after all"   he said
   "You think there're stars like that which behave like
firecrackers?"
   "Got me . . ."
   "If it was a firecracker"   I added   "it shouldn't
have twinkled like that"
   The policeman and I   stood there thinking it over
for a full five minutes
   "Even if was a star . . .   even if it was a firecracker . . ."
the policeman looked at his watch as he spoke   "Still,
what a strange case . . ."
   And the two of us turned to walk away

A young man I will just call "M" stuck a wire hoop at the end of a bamboo pole

I asked him what he was doing   and he told me that he was going to catch the crescent moon

I laughed   but you know   who would have imagined it?   Right there on the end of his pole he managed to snag the moon

Shouting "I got it! I got it!"   M went to grab the moon   but it was scalding hot so he dropped it on the floor with a "*Hot! Hot! Ouch!*"   He said "Sorry to bug you   but will you pass me that cup over there?"   When I gave it to him   he poured some fizzy soda into it

I asked him what he was going to do

"Put it in here, of course"

I told him that if he did Mr. Moon would die

"So what? Who cares?"   he responded   picking the crescent moon up between two pencils   and dropping it into the cup

PLOP!   And with that a cloud of strange purple smoke began to rise from the cup   It got into M's nostrils so he let out a big *hatchooooo!*   Next it was my turn to let out a *hatchoo!*   And with that the two of us dropped to the ground unconscious

By the time we came to   the clock told us it was after midnight   What's more we were surprised to see the crescent moon back trembling in the sky beyond the window

M looked back and forth between the hands of his watch and the moon with a quizzical expression When he noticed the cup sitting on the table he went pale   The contents of the cup were gone   other than some soda which looked a little yellower than before   M took it to examine under a lamp   then suddenly brought it to his mouth

"Stop! It's poison!"   He didn't heed my warning and drank the rest of the soda in a single *gulp*   And since then   M has been in this condition   you see?

But no matter how much I thought back over it the whole affair left me completely bewildered   so I went to my friend S   to tell him what happened

S listened from his desk chair [square], letting out an occasional "hmmm"   As I told the story   he grew incredulous

"You've got to be kidding"

I told him no   I had seen the whole thing with my own eyes

S asked   "Well then   was Mr. Moon shining in the sky that evening?"

I told him it was a beautiful moonlit night   the moon was bluish and pale

S took a drag on his cigar and blew a smoke ring   and burst out laughing   "Moonshine, my boy!"

You're probably wondering what the whole point of this story is, right?   Good question   I haven't been able to figure it out   I still don't know   so I was hoping I might get your opinion

Now   the time has come to say "*Bon soir!*"   Good night everyone!   No doubt your dreams tonight will be different than usual

© Kyōhei Sakaguchi

Kyōhei Sakaguchi

Listen for
the Perfume

translated by Sam Malissa

"I'M NOT A HUMAN BEING. I just have a human shape. I can't see that shape. I'm a simple vessel. But nothing is put inside me. I wait for nothing. No rain fills me up, there's nothing to ladle in. I'm just there. There's a bird perched on a branch. Not that I'm looking at it. I'm just there. Legs, move! Move those legs. Legs that don't belong to anyone. Not even to me. Which is why I'm the one moving them. I'm not being moved by anyone. Just watching the body. I'm the bird. I'm this rock over here. I'm not human. Don't look at me. I sing. It's not my song. I'm that person. He's not human. He's getting inside of me. I hold all his memories. Just for now. So ask whatever you want. You won't get a single answer. You don't get what you don't get. The bird, the same age as me, is listening to what I'm saying. Which is why I have bird wings. Out here, where there's nothing, you can hear the city's voice. Its voice carries. Coming from somewhere far away. It comes to me through the electric lines. I'm a telephone pole. I have to stay here. You all can run off to wherever. Just listen to me when you're there. You'll be able to hear me no matter how far you go. Listen for something. Don't listen for an answer, just listen to listen. You can hear all sorts of sounds. There's a rope. Or there was. Rain was falling. I shake my body and it makes a noise. The noise isn't words. It's a scent. There's a scent in the air. You must not smell it. Listen for it, that wafting perfume. Did you hear it? I didn't. I have no ears. I am not an ear. I'm not even a simple vessel. I gather. Look at the things I've gathered. I myself have no eyes. I am an eye. I'm not even an eye. The eye sees sound completely. It remembers the sound. I can't remember. I have no memory. I just know. I feel the scent. Though I feel it, I don't describe it. I don't move. I am here. A telephone pole. My head hurts. The pain has come. Just showed up out of nowhere. The pain is alive. It breathes. I have a body. My body is gone. My eye can see it. But none of you know. Where are you? Come out. Please come out. Here it comes. I can't see the walls; there are trees all around, their colors transparent. Come here come here, come-come-come! I'm not some sort of weirdo. I'm a sound. I make noise. Bang on a rock, on a boulder, on your skin, on your head, bang on whatever you have right there beside you. Bang-bang-bang! Go ahead, give it a whack. Come on, folks, let's all bang together! It doesn't need to be in unison. Just drum whenever you feel like it. Do you feel like it? Then give it a bang! See how the sky is full of birds? That's because you're looking. Because you looked. You did look! At the redness of the birds. That's why you're drawn to the color red. You eat red berries that grow on a tree. There's a bird watching you eat. Let's say it's just one bird. I become the bird. Right now, I become the bird and perform the gesture of eating the red berries. And then I begin. Starting right now. What about wings? Bring wings, go find some wings somewhere. Yes, you. You bring those wings. Doesn't matter where from. Doesn't matter what it is. Just bring whatever will work for wings. Hurry. I'll be gone. Any second now, I'm gone. Hurry. It's not a question of time. Faster. Go faster! Okay, calm down now. I'm a bird. Right now, before your very eyes, I'm a bird. I'm here. Now I perch on a big rock. From up here, higher than where I was, I start to sing. I sing only because I'm a bird, and I'm not human. I'm about to change. Because I sing. And now I'm a bird. I am not myself. I'm not human at all. I just have a human shape. But I can't see. Can't hear. I don't know. I don't think. All I do is sing. Can you hear my voice? Can you hear me out there? You sure did go far. Really far, didn't you. It's fine. If you're scared, listen like you're scared. When everyone else is gone, I'll still be singing. Just watch my changing shape. I can't see it for myself. But when I wake up, please, don't tell me about it. You can't tell me about it. Because I'm not human. Because I don't wake up. I'm always asleep. Deep, deep asleep. Still, I call myself myself. But it's a bird self. Because I sing."

When he opened his mouth, the man was a woman. The woman became a man, wearing something red, who knows where she found it. Up there on the rock the man, still as a woman, took the form of a bird. The mouth, still shaped like a beak, opened. And the insects came. They wanted to be eaten. One after the next the insects drew closer to the man's mouth. The man, pretending to be a woman, calling shrilly, thrust out his tongue and lapped up the bugs. His body convulsed. His ribs were clearly visible. The man was hungry. Skin and bones. Just when you thought

he was dozing in the hammock, he was up on his feet, aiming that queer screech at everyone. His hands were empty. He was just up there on the rock, working his legs. Hard black wood. Taut strings. The instrument was brought to the man. The bird looked on dubiously at this new object. At first it flew off. They came closer, and it fluttered away. Hid behind the big rock. It must have been frightened. But as it gradually understood there was no danger, it started to emerge, showing more of itself. Its hair was long. Down to its knees. Red hair. Body smeared with mud. Teeth bared, looking like it might bite at any second. Saliva dripped from its mouth. The man started to struggle. The insects filled his gullet, choking him, and he fell over. His body went rigid for some time. When everyone pressed in closer, his legs began to thrash. The people who were sure they shouldn't be frightened came even closer. Someone was attacked by the bird. Blood flowed. When the man's hair touched the ground it was pulled downward. Sucked into the dirt. The man sank up to his ankles. He wasn't going anywhere. The bird kept on screaming. Quietly, so that you had to strain to hear it properly. The man said, "It came, it's been here a while, it was right there, it is what it is, come inside, come in," and so saying he invited everyone in. No one moved, though. A few people who were tending to the bleeding one shouted for the man to stop. But the man, stuck in the mud to his knees, was violent. He hurled a length of wood with a sharpened end at us. He was out of breath but wouldn't stop struggling. "I'm a bird," he said quietly, "listen to my song," then shut his eyes tight. His body stilled. Quiet as a plant in the soil, the man was a bird. His hair was open. His red hair opened up to become wings. The wings unfurled, blown open by the wind, and the crowd formed a circle around the bird. The instrument was propped up against the man's body. The man took it and began to slowly sing. It was a quiet song. His teeth showed, and several were missing. Air whistled through the gaps. The man began telling the story of the bird. Perching on a branch. Being an eye. Having its partner devoured. The time it first experienced fruit. The time it left the forest behind. They were no longer in the forest. Nonetheless, the man sang the bird's song. He kept singing and singing, never stopping. I have no idea how long it went on. The man showed no signs of tiring. Beginning, beginning, beginning, beginning. Everyone kept nodding and murmuring to the word *beginning*. At some point it became like a chant accompanying the music. Gradually, the group and the bird became one. Several people trimmed the man's long hair, spread it wide, and he sang about the bird in flight. It passed by a handful of clouds. The women undressed and played the part of the air. The bird seemed to expect this—on that day, at that place, the man would sing. There were no birds in the sky. No birds around anywhere. Just red earth. They were getting far away from the encampment. The day must have been over. And then the man started singing the morning song.

The morning is ever before me
The front door always knows the dream
I've flown, my legs are tied, still on the ground
Flew at top speed, saw only things I had forgotten
The bird has fallen, fallen into a hole, seen a moon
    that looks like time
The folded forest is there, the bird rests its wings
The gathered waters were fish, the fish spoke with
    the bird
What's that there? Even the stones at the bottom
    joined in
It's getting darker, the morning grows dark
The morning is endlessly becoming me
The things I've seen are right there
The bird became the water, the fish became the stones
How far back should I go?
Where is my original form?
Two strangers asked the fish
The fish didn't answer
The fish was water
The water was surprised
The bird listened
Listened to the sound
The morning had
Had a dream
It was the bird
It had a dream
Water is bird
Fish is stone

Wings are gone
Ahh, terrifying
Ahh, delightful
Ahh
Ahh
Rain fell
Bird died
Water moved
Stones vanished
Insects flew
Soil shakes
Song weeps
I am
bird 🐵

Note from the translator: This is a translation of Section 55 of the 2016 novel *Ducking Under the Eaves to Watch Reality Pass By*. The Japanese title, *Genjitsu yadori,* is a play on the common phrase *amayadori,* taking shelter from the rain. For the author, this is about more than just staying dry: it's a shift in perspective. In comments on the title he said that when you duck under the eaves of a building to wait out the rain, your attitude toward the rain changes. It had been pelting you but now it's a curtain protecting you from the world. Before, it was a threat and now it's an object of fascination and meditation as you wait for it to pass, gently enveloping you in the meantime. He wanted to apply the same idea to reality, exploring how his perception of it might change if he could duck out and observe.

From the modern Japanese
translation by Seikō Itō

———

TAKASAGO
A Noh Play

translated and with an introduction
by Jay Rubin

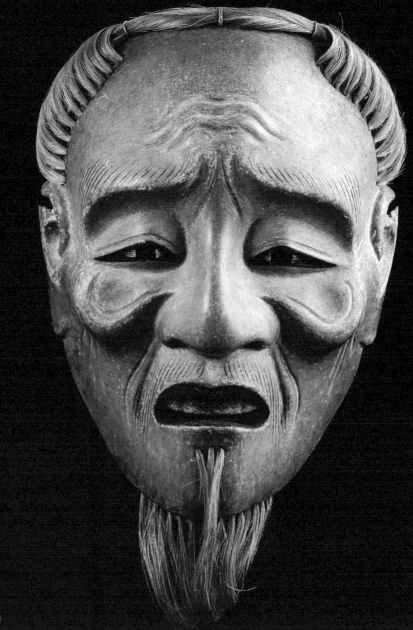

© Yoshiaki Kanda

SONG OF THE EARTH:
AN INTRODUCTION

FOUR OUT OF THE FIVE plays in a full Noh program deal with dark themes such as vengeance, longing, jealousy, and horror, presented in a Buddhistic context peopled by ghosts unable to detach themselves from earthly suffering. The first of the five plays, however, is traditionally a Shinto piece that embraces all that is good in life, and the supernatural beings who appear on stage are not ghosts but gods who encourage us to experience the world with gratitude. In contrast to the Buddhist view, which sees the world as nothing but an illusion, Shinto encourages us to savor life joyfully with all five senses.

Takasago celebrates sound. It starts with the proposition that all of nature is alive and singing, and it goes from there to build a logic of celebration that goes something like this: All things in nature, both animate and seemingly inanimate, have heart. Heart is the one indispensable element of poetry. All the sounds of nature are, in themselves, poems. Poetry, as part of nature, is eternal. The sound of the wind in the pines is an eternal poem. Poetry is a holy balm that softens the pain of life and unites the hearts of husband and wife into old age under a benevolent ruler. The wind in the pines is the sound of two gods, husband and wife, expressing their eternal love for each other. All of this is to be celebrated with energetic song and dance.

The finale of *Takasago* is a full-fledged production number in which the old god of the first act reveals himself in his true youthful form and then dances, surrounded by dancing girls (in the text, that is, but with lots of lively music). They dance in praise of poetry and marriage and the benevolent rule of the emperor and good fortune and long life, the whole universe united in praise of the poetry of the wind in the pines. Everything is alive and contributing equally to the joyful noise of the universe.

Aural images are strategically placed in the play. Early on, it is pointedly noted that there is too much mist on the shore for you to see the waves, but you can surely *hear* them. An evening bell tolls in the distance—twice. Insects cry. The dancing girls sing. The wind is heard swishing onomatopoetically through the pines in the very last line, and even grass, sand, and water have their sounds. The performance underscores all this by bringing in a third drummer and letting the musicians make a great commotion reminiscent of a Shinto festival.

Not that the play is all uncritical optimism. The initial view we have of the old couple featured in the play suggests a dark side to longevity. The pair have outlived their friends and find themselves spending wakeful nights alone, their one source of comfort at such moments being feelings shared in poetry. Their apparently endless raking of the pine needles is ambiguous: is it a symbol of the pine's continual renewal, or sheer drudgery as they drag themselves through old age? Perhaps the presentation itself is the answer: the old couple in their muted earth-colored costumes, he with his rake and she with her broom, is an image of quiet, dignified beauty. Small wonder that verses from the play are traditionally sung at weddings and that the image of the old couple is a beloved icon that finds its way into many Japanese homes in the form of dolls and paintings.

The play is set precisely in historical time. The action takes place during the Engi era (901–923), which is when the first imperial anthology of poetry, the *Kokinshū,* was compiled (in the year 905). Instead of the usual anonymous traveling Buddhist monk who appears to begin the action, we have a Shinto priest named Tomonari, modeled on a man who actually lived during the Engi era.

Like other Noh travelers, though, Tomonari encounters a mystery—in fact, two mysteries. He sees the old couple raking needles under the Takasago pine and asks them why this pine and a pine in Sumiyoshi (or Suminoe), several days' journey away, should be known as the "Twin Pines." The old man compounds the mystery by replying that he himself is from distant Sumiyoshi, while his wife lives here in Takasago, and he urges her to explain. Before she can answer, Tomonari expresses his surprise that such an apparently long-wedded old couple should live so far from each other. The woman chides him for his foolish question and declares, "A man and wife may be separated by 10,000 leagues of rivers and mountains, but there is no distance between them when their hearts are truly in touch."

There follows a lengthy sung disquisition that rejects Buddhism's distinction between sentient beings with a potential for salvation and insentient beings for which salvation is irrelevant: "People say that plants and trees have no heart, but still they never fail to flower and bear fruit at the correct times, and blossoms naturally open first from branches on the south side of the tree when the warmth of spring arrives . . . Grass and trees, soil and sand, voice of wind and sound of water: there is a heart that each and every one of them contains."

The old man and woman then disclose their true identities: "We are the spirits of the Twin Pines of Takasago and Suminoe revealed in human form as man and wife," after which they board a fishing boat and sail across the evening waves to far-off Sumiyoshi, inviting the others to join them. Tomonari and his companions follow in their own boat, and in Sumiyoshi witness the spectacle of the young god's dance.

And so the mystery of the Twin Pines is solved: the same spirit that unites a man and woman in marriage, that makes it a point of celebration for the two of them to grow old together, whatever the hardships, is what unites the trees. It is the communion of hearts achieved through poetry, through song, through sound.

THIS TRANSLATION of novelist Seikō Itō's modern Japanese rendering of Zeami's fifteenth-century text first appeared in the February 2021 issue of the magazine *Shinchō,* where it benefitted greatly from the attention of Maho Adachi and other members of the editorial staff.

TAKASAGO

COME, LET US GO NOW, binding the cords of our travel cloaks, cords as long as the endless days ahead of us.

I who speak these words am Tomonari, chief priest of the Aso Shrine in Higo. Never having seen the imperial capital, Kyoto, it dawned on me one day to travel there. And, since it is on the way, I wish to have a look at the Takasago shore in Harima.

Preparing for our spring journey, we proceed with spring in our steps down the road that stretches like a length of fabric toward the distant capital. As decisively as we cut the cloth for our travel robes, we make up our minds to leave this very day, launching our boat from the shore. With soft spring breezes sweeping all around us, how many days have we been traveling on our tranquil sea route? Before we know it, we have reached our destination, which had once seemed to be so far beyond the clouds— yes, here we are at Takasago on Harima's shore, the bay of Takasago.

Tomonari says,

"We have traveled so swiftly that we have already arrived in Takasago. If a local person should happen by, I wish to ask him the story of the famous pine."

His attendant replies,

"Yes, let us do so, Your Reverence."

At which point they hear two aged voices:

"The sun goes down in Takasago, the spring breeze whispers in the pines, and the bell on the hill resounds."

Mist rises on the shore, and we can no longer see the waves.

"Only by their sound can we tell the ebb and flow of the tide."

The voice continues,

"We wish there were someone left alive who knows us well, but not even the long-lived pine of Takasago is a friend from our youth."

Countless months and days have passed, and now our hair has turned white as if snow had piled upon our heads. Like ancient cranes left alone in their nest, we wake on frosty spring nights to see the moon lingering in the sky at dawn, hearing nothing day after day but the wind in the pines, our hearts our only friends as we lay out our loneliness in poetry as if spreading a mat of woven sedge.

We pine for someone to visit us, but all we hear is the sea breeze whispering in the pines. Let us press our sleeves, flecked with fallen pine needles, against our rake and broom and sweep away the needles that litter the ground beneath the Takasago pine.

Their voices continue to blend:

"The Onoe pine, here in Takasago, has seen the passage of many years, and we have become deeply wrinkled as the waves of age wash over us. Old as we are, how long can we go on living as we rake and sweep the needles beneath the trees? The Iki Living Pine is yet another tree that has been famous here since ages past."

The Shinto priest Tomonari says:

"You, aged sir, may I ask you a question?"

"Are you speaking to me? What question do you have for me?"

"Which of these trees might be the Takasago Pine?"

"It is this one beneath which we are now sweeping needles."

"The Takasago and Suminoe Pines are famous as the 'Twin Pines,' which usually means two trees have grown from a single root. But Takasago and Sumiyoshi are so far apart, they are in different provinces. How can two such widely separated trees possibly be known as the Twin Pines?"

"Yes, you are right, the preface to Japan's first imperially commissioned poetry anthology, the *Kokinshū,* says clearly that 'The pines of Takasago and Suminoe seem to be twins.' I, however, live in Sumiyoshi in the province of Settsu, while this old woman is from here in Takasago. Tell him what you know about this, Old Girl."

The priest says with feeling,

"How mysterious! This aged couple look to be man and wife, and yet he says that they live a province apart, separated by shore and mountain, he in Suminoe, she in Takasago. How can this be?"

To which the old woman replies,

"What a foolish thing to say! A man and wife may be separated by 10,000 leagues of rivers and mountains, but there is no distance between them when their hearts are truly in touch."

"Just think about it," the old man says.

The pines of Takasago and Suminoe are trees devoid of hearts, and yet are they not said to be twins? How much more so should it be true of human beings with feelings! This old man has made his way here to Takasago daily, year after year, from distant Sumiyoshi, growing closer all the while to his old wife until, along with the pines, this married couple are said to be twins.

"How engrossing your words are! And the Twin Pines I asked about earlier: has anything about them been handed down in this place?" the priest asks.

"The people of long ago called them a symbol of an auspicious reign," the aged couple say.

"Takasago stood for that ancient age when the oldest collection of Japanese poetry, the *Man'yōshū,* was compiled," says the wife.

"And Sumiyoshi signifies the present age called Engi, ruled over by His Majesty . . ."

. . . while the pines tell of the inexhaustible leaves of words, flourishing equally now and of old in praise of the reign.

"The more I hear, the more welcome are your words. Now all my doubts have cleared on this clear spring day."

"Like the Buddha's own appearance, the light is soft that bathes the western sea."

"Over there in Suminoe,"

"And here in Takasago,"

"The pines are vivid in their hue."

"The spring . . ."

So tranquil, the seas calm all around us, the realm at peace, the breezes—gentle as the season—stir not the boughs under this, His Majesty's reign. How blessed are we and blessed, too, the twin pines, to have lived in such a reign. Yes, truly, folk like us are fortunate to live in an age so marvelous that no praise can ever do it full justice. Oh, how great the favor bestowed on us by His Majesty! How great his sheer beneficence!

The priest Tomonari asks the old couple raking pine needles,

"Please be so good as to tell me more about the Takasago pine."

The old man replies,

"People say that plants and trees have no heart, but still they never fail to flower and bear fruit at the correct times, and the blossoms naturally open first from branches on the south side of the tree when the warmth of spring arrives."

And yet this pine's appearance remains forever unchanged, forever green.

Though the four seasons may come in turn, the color of the pine lasts beyond a thousand years, its green only deepening amid the snow. And in that thousand years, the pine blooms only once, they say, flowering ten times altogether.

"Pining for this opportunity, the branches of the pine . . ."

. . . are bejeweled with dewdrops gathered on the countless leaves of words, which give radiance to the hearts of all.

"Yes, every living thing,"

we hear, follows our land's Way of Poetry.

The old man continues:

As Fujiwara no Chōnō has said, the voices of all things on earth, both animate and inanimate, are themselves poems. Grass and trees, soil and sand, voice of wind and sound of water: there is a heart that each and every one of them contains. Both the spring forest stirring in the eastern breeze and the autumn insects crying in the north wind's dew: are they not in form already poems? he asks. Of all trees, the pine is noblest, for its name is written with a character composed of three elements meaning "ten," "eight," and "lord." Ever brimming with greenness, its color has remained unchanged from antiquity to our own day, and it has been praised by all at home and abroad from the time it was granted court rank by Qin Shi Huang, the first emperor of China.

The old man also says:

"High on the hill, the bell of Takasago now tolls."

Though frost forms on them in the morning, however many years pass by, the needles of the pine remain deep green. Morning and evening we sweep needles beneath the tree, but they are inexhaustible. For truly, as the *Kokinshū* tells us, "The needles of the pine do not scatter until all are gone." Their color continues on and on, increasing. How natural that the pine should be seen as a metaphor for a long reign, along with the *masaki* vine cited in the *Kokinshū* preface! Among the evergreens that tell of such longevity, the Takasago pine is famous as a symbol of ages to come. The Twin Pines are auspicious!

Tomonari calls out to the aged couple:

"This famous pine, the branches of this much-praised pine reveal the ages through which it has lived. So, too, I ask you to reveal your true selves and speak your names to me."

To which they reply:

"What, then, should we conceal? We are the spirits of the Twin Pines of Takasago and Suminoe revealed in human form as man and wife."

How marvelous! The noted pines have shown us an omen.

"Plants and trees have no heart," the couple say together.

But insofar as this is an auspicious reign,

"Both earth and trees—"

—belong to our great lord's country, where it will always be *sumiyoshi,* or good to live.

"We shall go ahead to Sumiyoshi and wait for you there," says the old man, and they hasten aboard a fishing boat anchored in the evening waves on shore. Letting a tailwind propel the craft, they head out to sea, yes, the old ones have gone out to sea.

Kyōgen interlude

THE PRIEST CALLS to his attendants:

"Is someone present?"

"I am here before you, Your Reverence."

"Go and bring someone who lives on this shore."

"Yes, Your Reverence. . . . Is there someone here who lives on this shore?"

To which a person responds—

"I hear he is asking for someone who lives here. I think I'll go and find out what he wants. . . . Well, then, I understand you are looking for someone who lives on this shore. How can I be of service?"

"My master says he has a little something he wants to ask you. Please come with me."

"I understand."

"Your Reverence, I have brought along someone who lives on this shore."

"I am here in your presence, Your Reverence. "

"I am Tomonari, chief priest of the Aso Shrine in Kyushu's Higo Province, having come to this shore for the very first time. Please tell me what you know about this Takasago pine."

"This is a truly unexpected request. I do live here, but I have no detailed knowledge of what you ask, which is better known to high-ranking people. Still, having been summoned as a resident of the area, it would be unseemly of me to reply that I know nothing, and so I will do my best to tell you everything that I have heard."

"Yes, please do so."

"First of all, let me say that, on this shore, we have long referred to this pine tree as the Takasago pine. Now, as to the 'twin' part about two trees growing from the same root. That has been said, I have heard, because in the preface of the *Kokinshū* it is written: 'The Takasago and Suminoe pines seem to be twins.' Among the many kinds of trees, the pine is an evergreen that retains its glory for many years, and thus the Way of Poetry is said to have been likened to the Takasago and Suminoe pines—the words of song as numberless as the needles on these two trees.

"One view holds that the deity of Takasago and the deity of Sumiyoshi are husband and wife. Thus, when the god of this shrine visits Sumiyoshi, the couple engage in conversation at the base of the pine tree there, and likewise when the god of Sumiyoshi visits here, they converse at the base of this pine. From long ago through our present day, they have been visiting each other like that, and so it has apparently long been said among us lowly inhabitants of this shore that the pines of Takasago and Sumiyoshi are twins.

"In any case, the god of this shrine and the god of Sumiyoshi are but a single god incarnate, and thus we say it is entirely due to the spiritual power of the two shrines' gods that the Way of Poetry continues to flourish and husbands and wives remain close to the end. As the words of the poems themselves tell us, even if grains of sand were to grow into massive boulders and dust were to pile up into mountains and the numberless sands of the beach were to run out, the words we recite in poetry will never run out—or so I have been told, though in fact I do not know the true meaning of the 'twin' in Twin Pines.

"Regarding pines, however, they say that once a pine grows but a single inch, its greenery becomes eternal. It will live a thousand—nay, ten thousand—years, and there is nothing more auspicious. And because the two gods are said to have planted the two trees, the twin pines are also called the Pines Planted Together. I have heard, too, that they will protect this land of ours for another 5,670,000,000 years, until the Bodhisattva Maitreya comes to save the world.

"This, then, is all that I have heard, but tell me, please, why do you wish to know the story of the Twin Pines?"

"Thank you for your painstaking account. Before meeting you, we encountered an aged couple, and when we asked them about the Takasago pine, they recounted the story in great detail much as you have done, after which they said they would wait for us in Sumiyoshi and leaped aboard a skiff that was anchored by the shore, sailing out to sea until we lost sight of them."

"How amazing to hear you say that! I do believe that the god of Sumiyoshi must have come to visit this shrine as I mentioned earlier, and he must have spoken to you while he and the god of Takasago were together sweeping needles beneath the tree."

The man of the shore continues—

"And if, in addition, they said they would wait for you in Sumiyoshi as they boarded a skiff on the shore and sailed out to sea, then I believe you must make a pilgrimage to the Sumiyoshi Shrine without delay. I happen to have a skiff that I recently finished building but have not yet taken on its maiden voyage. For such an event, I was hoping to have a worthy passenger, and now if I can welcome aboard one who is not only the chief priest of the Aso Shrine but also so blessed as to have exchanged words with the gods of Takasago and Sumiyoshi themselves, then I will be able to look forward to many years of fortunate sailing. So please board my brand-new boat. I shall ply the oar and accompany you to Sumiyoshi myself."

"So, then, everyone, let us climb aboard and sail to Sumiyoshi."

"Oh, see what is happening! Thanks to the will of the gods, a tailwind of added strength has miraculously sprung up! Please hurry and board, everyone!"

"Yes, let us do so."

AND SO THEIR craft makes its propitious departure.

From this Takasago shore, we raise our sail, yes, raise our sail, and journey with the rising moon, the tide rising, the waves foaming as we pass the foam-flecked isle of Awaji looming in the distance, distant Naruo too goes by, and speedily have we arrived in Suminoe, yes, here we are in Suminoe already.

Whereupon the god of Sumiyoshi in youthful form appears and begins to sing and dance.

His Majesty the Emperor once sang, "Long years have passed since we first saw the princess pine on Sumiyoshi shore: indeed, through how many ages has she lived?" To which I, the god of Sumiyoshi, sang in reply, "That princess pine and I are a loving couple, did you not know? Age after age from long ago."

Oh, priests of the shrine, play your sacred night music, striking your drums in time to comfort all the gods!

The priestly musicians increase the fervor of their playing.

From the waves of Aoki-ga-hara in the western sea, sings the god,

"The godly pine has risen! Perhaps because spring has come, the remaining snows lie thin upon Asaka Beach."

"On the shore we harvest beautiful seaweed,"

"And if we brush our hips against the pine tree's base,"

Eternal green fills our hands.

"If I break off a spray of plum and tuck it in my hair,"

Spring snow seems to fall upon my robe.

O blessed revelation! O blessed advent of the god! How precious to worship this vision of the dancing Sumiyoshi god beneath the clear [*sumi*] full moon!

"Truly, many dancing maidens appear with him, their voices also clear, as the waves reflect the Suminoe pine. Surely this is what is known as the Dance of the Blue Ocean Waves."

Straight, too, is the Way of both God and Emperor, and if we can go straight to spring in the capital,

"That, indeed, is the dance known as Return to the Palace."

Now hoping for His Majesty to be with us always, "And donning the robes to worship the god,"

We dance with arms waving outward to sweep away demons, then draw arms inward to embrace good fortune. Playing "Music of a Thousand Autumns," we heal the people, and dancing to the "Music of Ten Thousand Years," we pray for His Majesty's longevity. The wind sweeps through the Twin Pines, rustling the branches with a joyful, refreshing sound like that of dancers' sleeves brushing against each other.

How much we enjoy this refreshing sound! 🐵

Note from the translator: After the Kyōgen interlude, the emphasis shifts decisively from what Zeami called the "ear-opening" (*kaimon*) part of the play, in which verbal content is central, to the "eye-opening" (*kaigen*) conclusion, in which the focus is on the actor's dance, and the text does little more than describe his movements. Not only do "The priestly musicians increase the fervor of their playing," but the actual musicians onstage provide an accompaniment of special vigor. *Takasago* is often performed in January to celebrate the most important holiday of the year.

Eight Modern Haiku Poets on Music

selected and translated by Andrew Campana

Takako Hashimoto (1899–1963)

中空に音の消えてゆくつばな笛
its sound
vanishing in midair—
reed grass flute

目つむれば鉦と鼓のみや壬生念仏
if you close your eyes
all that's left are gongs and drums—
Mibu Temple festival

夏雲の立ちたつ伽藍童女うた
summer clouds
surrounding the temple
a little girl singing

祭太鼓うちてやめずもやまずあれ
festival drums
keep playing and playing
I wish they'd never stop

祭笛吹くとき男佳かりける
a man
playing a flute at the festival
is incredibly attractive

踊り唄終りを始めにくりかへし
a song to dance to
its end repeats
at its beginning

髪白く笛息ふかきまつりびと
a festival-goer
despite his white hair
plays the flute so powerfully

踊り唄遠しそこよりあゆみ来て
the dancing song
is so distant now
I didn't realize how far I'd gone

炎天下鉦が冴え音のチンドン屋
under the blazing sun
cymbals sound brilliantly clear—
chindon-ya marching band

太鼓の音とびだす祇園囃子より
the sound of a taiko drum
leaps out
from the music of the Gion Festival

蘆の笛吹きあひて音を異にする
reed flutes
try to play in harmony
but each sounds different

露万朶幼きピアノの音が飛ぶ飛ぶ
branches covered in scattered dew
the sound of a child at the piano
playing notes at random

指さえざえ笛の高音の色かへて
my fingers
can so clearly change the tone
of the flute's high notes

をどりの輪つよし男ゐて女ゐて
such a strong ring of dancers
all of the men
and all of the women!

かの老婆まためぐりくるをどりくる
that old woman
has come around dancing
and around and around again

尽きぬをどりおきて帰るや来た道を
the dance is seemingly never-ending
so I leave them to it
and head back home

伏眼の下笛一文字に冴え高音
under downcast eyes
the flutist plays a single note
high and clear

雪の駅ピアノ木箱を地膚の上
snowy train station
wooden piano crate
lying on the bare earth

Dakotsu Iida (1885–1962)

琴の音や芭蕉すなはち初嵐
the sound of the koto
or is that the banana tree?
the first storm of autumn

かたよりて田歌にすさむ女房かな
there's nothing
these women get into more
than rice-planting songs

髪梳けば琴書のちりや浅き春
combing my hair
looking at the koto and books lying all around—
the beginning of spring

鈴の音のかすかにひびく日傘かな
the sound of a bell
faintly echoing
in my parasol

やまがつのうたへば鳴るや皐月川
mountain folk sing
and it roars back—
rain-swollen summer river

新月に牧笛をふくわらべかな
a child
blowing a shepherd's pipe
at the new moon

三月の雲のひかりに植林歌
under the glow
of the March clouds
a tree planting song

こたへなき雪山宙に労働歌
left unanswered
hanging in the snowy mountain air
a working song

つかのまの絃歌ひびきて秋の海
for just a moment
strings and voices echo over
the autumn sea

うたひめにネオンかはたれはつしぐれ
a lady singer
in neon light at dusk—
first rains of autumn

茶房昼餐祈禱歌冬のこだませり
lunch at a teahouse
songs of prayer
echoed by winter

Hekigotō Kawahigashi (1873–1937)

曲すみし笛の余音や春の月
the sound of a flute lingers
after the song is over—
spring moon

野に遊ぶ歌に行人唱和かな
someone in a field
is peacefully singing
and a passerby joins in!

田移りの早乙女が唄を森隔つ
rice-planting women
move from paddy to paddy
their songs echoing from across the forest

舞殿や薫風昼の楽起る
from the shrine hall
music drifting
on the summer breeze

麦笛を吹く曇り出した風のそひ来る
someone is playing a barley flute
the cloud-bringing wind
comes to play along

芝居茶屋を出てマントを正す口に唄出る
leaving the teahouse after a kabuki play
I adjust my cloak
as a song emerges from my mouth

Fura Maeda (1884–1954)

春月や謡をうたふ僧と僧
spring moon—
monks
singing to other monks

踊見る色傘しづむおかぼ畑
watching the dance
of colorful umbrellas
sinking into the dry rice fields

はるかなる秋の海より海女の口笛
from the distant
autumn sea
the whistling of a pearl diver

勧進の鈴ききぬ春も遠からじ
I heard the bells
of the temple fundraiser—
spring must not be far

落葉松に高音鶯うしろ向き
in the larch tree
a high-pitched nightingale
facing away from me

虫鳴くや向ひ合ひたる寺の門
insects singing
two temple gates
facing one another

Hisajo Sugita (1890–1946)

帰省子の琴のしらべをきく夜かな
my daughter is finally home
I'll spend all evening
listening to her playing the koto

上つ瀬に歌劇明りや河鹿きく
upstream
I see the lights from the opera house
while listening to kajika frogs

吹き習ふ麦笛の音はおもしろや
the sound of someone
learning to play the barley flute—
so charming!

さみし身にピアノ鳴り出よ秋の暮
let the piano ring out
for my lonely self—
autumn dusk

クリスマス近づく寮の歌稽古
Christmas approaches—
from the dormitory
I hear a choir rehearsal

よそに鳴る夜長の時計数へけり
I spent a long night
counting the hours chimed by the clock
in someone else's house

Awajijo Takahashi (1890–1955)

我が門やよその子遊ぶ手毬唄
at my gate
playing with a temari ball
other people's children singing

風鈴に起きて寝ざめのよき子かな
what a good child
to wake up to the sound
of wind chimes!

笛の音や泣きみ怒りみ祭獅子
the sound of the flute—
startling children into fury and tears
at the lion dance festival

麦笛を吹く子が居りぬ麦の中
there was a child
blowing a barley flute
amidst the barley

Shizunojo Takeshita (1887–1951)

弾つ放して誰そ我がピアノ夏埃
who played my piano
and left it open?
summer dust

的礫や風鈴に来る葦の風
shining bright as wet gravel
the breeze from the reeds
reaches the wind chimes

鍵板打つや指紋鮮かに夏埃
striking the keyboard
leaving clear prints
in the summer dust

瑞葦に風鈴吊りて棲家とす
hanging a wind chime
on a fresh reed—
making a home

八ツ手散る楽譜の音符散る如く
paperplant flowers scatter
like notes falling
from sheet music

Arō Usuda (1879–1951)

夕花菜帰漁の唄のはずみ来よ
yellow evening blossoms
the fisherman's song propelling them
come home!

寒行太鼓時にみだるる月吹く夜
monks playing drums for winter training
fall out of time—
a night with a wind-blown moon

落日の枯野ゆく子のうたへるや
sunset
on a withered field
a child passes by singing

風の声碧天に舞ふ木の葉かな
the voice of the wind—
tree leaves dancing
in the clear blue sky

———————

Note from the translator: I would like to express deep gratitude to Miyao Sakamoto—an award-winning haiku poet and author of books on Hisajo Sugita and Shizunojo Takeshita—for her insights on several of the haiku.

TAKAKO HASHIMOTO (1899–1963) is the pen name of Tama Hashimoto, born in Tokyo. She was highly influential as one of the first women to include herself as an active presence within her verses. She originally began to write haiku under the guidance of Hisajo Sugita, also featured in this volume.

 DAKOTSU IIDA (1885–1962) is the pen name of Takeji Iida, born in the village of Gonari (now part of Fuefuki city) in Yamanashi prefecture. Yamanashi's landscapes provided the setting for his poetry throughout his life. He received enormous acclaim as a haiku poet for his grand, classically inspired style—unusual in modern haiku—and was even called "the modern Bashō."

 HEKIGOTŌ KAWAHIGASHI (1873–1937) is the pen name of Heigorō Kawahigashi, born in the city of Matsuyama on the island of Shikoku. He was one of the main students of Shiki Masaoka, the founder of modern haiku, and pushed his followers to innovate the form even beyond what he accomplished. He was also a prolific travel writer.

 FURA MAEDA (1884–1954) is the pen name of Chūkichi Maeda, born in Tokyo. Not only was he widely acknowledged as one of the most prominent haiku poets of the Taisho era (1912–1926), but also he was a well-known newspaper reporter and later a bureau chief.

 HISAJO SUGITA (1890–1946) is the pen name of Hisa Sugita, born in Kagoshima on Kyushu. She founded *Hanagoromo,* a journal for women haiku poets, to foster a new generation of women in a largely male-dominated literary form. Her turbulent personal life made her the subject of many novels, plays, and television dramas in the decades after her death.

 AWAJIJO TAKAHASHI (1890–1955) is the pen name of Sumi Takahashi, born on Cape Wada in Hyogo prefecture. She was a member of the haiku coterie Unmo ("Mica"), and became well known for writing haiku that captured the atmosphere of Edo-period work.

 SHIZUNOJO TAKESHITA (1887–1951) is the pen name of Shizuno Takeshita, born in the village of Hieda in Fukuoka prefecture, now part of the city of Yukuhashi. She was a schoolteacher and a poet, and her haiku quickly became known for promoting women's independence. She was a key member of the haiku coterie Hototogisu ("Cuckoo"), whose titular periodical remains the most prominent and longest-running haiku journal.

 ARŌ USUDA (1879–1951) is the pen name of Uichirō Usuda, born in Komoro village (now a city) in Nagano prefecture. In the 1910s, he pushed against movements to reform haiku that were beginning to dominate the form, aiming to keep it as a kind of folk poetry in the tradition of Bashō.

Tomoka Shibasaki

———

A man opens a cafe
in a shopping arcade,
dreaming that it
will become like the
jazz cafe he used to
frequent as a student;
the cafe is open
for nearly thirty years,
then closes down

translated by Polly Barton

THE CAFE WAS on the third corner of the old shopping arcade.

The building itself was pretty ramshackle, and in the showcase outside, the plastic models of cream soda, pancakes, sandwiches, and so on had faded and acquired a layer of dust. The external door and the walls were plastered with numerous little boards depicting menu items. Coffee in a plain cup and saucer, curry and rice with a serving of fukujinzuke pickles on the side, shaved ice in the summer and azuki bean porridge in the winter—the simple illustrations, which could hardly be called well-rendered, were drawn by the cafe owner in thick marker pen. The prices were written in red.

Most days, mornings brought a series of two or three elderly men at a time, who would spread out their sports papers—newspapers that featured a range of sports, entertainment, and celebrity news. Come lunchtime, the space would grow lively with the sound of women talking.

The dilapidated old cafe had once been new. When it first opened, the plastic models of food were brightly colored, and the sign outside with the coffee company logo lit up as it was supposed to. The cafe's owner was young, too. Or, more accurately, he was approaching forty. He'd just quit his job at an office supplies company, where he'd worked for almost two decades, and started up the cafe of his dreams.

The cafe was modeled on one the owner had frequented as a student in Tokyo. Positioned midway between the station and the university, the cafe played jazz, and students who were into music and films sat in there for hours. Its wooden walls had turned a caramel color and the tables were riddled with scratches. A jumble of magazines and works of foreign literature filled the shelves. In his student days, the owner had stopped in at the cafe at least twice a week. He'd fallen for a girl working there, but graduated and left town without ever telling her how he felt.

When he decided to leave his job, he returned to the place he grew up and opened his cafe in the shopping arcade outside the station, which he'd passed through every day until he finished high school. At busy times his wife, a classmate from high school, helped him out. People from his year at school who'd remained in the area came by, sometimes bringing their friends, and as a result, the business got off to a reasonable start.

The area was one where few people went to university. Most of the owner's middle school classmates had gone on to work in factories along the coast or taken over the family business. There was a dignity about these people, who seemed so well-suited to their jobs in the dried goods shop or the ironmonger in the arcade or one of the small factories in the area. They spoke of the cafe owner, who'd gone to university and had a taste for European films and jazz, as something of an oddball.

The owner's dad would complain to those around him that, after sending his son to university, he'd wound up running a cafe. With scorn, he would describe his son's new venture as part of the "water trade," a general term for the entertainment business, including its less reputable parts. "Yes," his son would counter, smiling, "the water we're using is top quality, we're doing a great water trade."

The owner's father died ten years previously, without once visiting his son's cafe. He'd even avoided passing in front of it. He'd been in hospital for a year before his death, and during that time the owner went back and forth between the cafe and the hospital. His two children found jobs and moved to more convenient locations. His wife started volunteering as a conversation partner for local elderly people.

The cafe had veered far from the owner's original dream. To suit his customers, it was now sports papers and baseball manga that lined its shelves. Told that the cafe's exterior wasn't very approachable, not the sort of place that someone ventured into off the street, he began out of desperation to draw pictures of coffee and curry on bits of board, which soon became a hit with the locals. He'd made more and more of these boards, sticking them up outside, until before long the cafe was featured on the local news channel as a "quirky spot," and that description stuck. Somehow, he became closer with his old schoolmates, whom he'd found hard to get along with when he was younger. It was actually quite fun running this kind of cafe, even if it wasn't what he'd initially intended, he'd think to himself. The one thing he didn't change was his commitment to playing the music that he wanted, although unlike the cafe of his student days, he played CDs, not records.

Nowadays, over half the shops in the arcade were closed. He was often reminded of a term he'd heard in a rakugo performance, back when he was young: shimotaya, or ex-shop. This arcade was lined with shimotaya, which were now used as houses. The older locals who frequented the cafe would moan about the situation, putting it down to the fact that young people these days wouldn't come to somewhere so unexciting. Another reason the arcade had gone to seed, though, was that many landlords didn't want to rent out shops, thinking it was more trouble than it was worth. In any case, the average age of his customers had certainly risen.

The arcade was welcomed with open arms when it first came along, but now the awning made the street feel dingy and deserted even during the day. For a long time, the cafe with all the pictures outside served as a landmark in navigating the space.

Another decade passed, and the old cafe closed down.

At this time, the cafe near the university in Tokyo, which the owner used to frequent, was still in business. A woman who'd worked there part-time as a student took over the business at age twenty-seven. The previous owner had worked nonstop in the cafe until he was eighty-two, when he finally took the decision to relax and listen to his records at home in the suburbs.

The young female owner didn't alter the place at all. She kept the battered walls, the bookshelves by the window, the chairs with ripped cushions and the menu all exactly as they were. Even the torn poster on the wall stayed put. It was a student band poster from long before her time. She had once asked the former owner what the band members were up to now. Yeah, I wonder, he had replied, disinterestedly. Did they come here often, the young woman had followed up. I guess they must have done, if the poster's up on the wall. It seemed the former owner's memory was growing dim. She supposed that if every year brought an influx of new students, and that a similar number would leave at the same time, and that process was repeated for decades, then it stood to reason that you wouldn't remember them all. With this thought, the young owner didn't ask any more questions. The former owner spoke very rarely about the past. He just brewed coffee and made toast in silence, playing his records, day in, day out.

When the former owner left, he took his records home with him, so the sole thing that did change about the cafe was the music.

The young owner was into music. She was interested in various genres, from many different countries and time periods, so the cafe now played a real assortment of tunes.

As she stood behind the counter surveying the floor, it often struck the new owner that the cafe seemed like an entirely different space depending on what music was playing. Nothing had changed, and yet those same walls that had been there for decades would seem to take on a different color. Time after time, the owner experienced how music, invisible to the eye, would spread through the air, changing everything about the place.

One hot summer evening, she put on some Kawachi Ondo, a type of folk music from the Osaka area. A friend whom she'd been going to concerts and festivals with since her student days had recommended her a particular song.

She had neither a CD nor a record of said song, so she played the video on her smartphone, which she hooked up to the speakers. She'd grown up in an apartment in the city center, and, never having taken part in the traditional Bon Odori dance when Kawachi Ondo was played, the rhythm and the singing voices were utterly new to her. It was energetic yet laid-back, the kind of music that instantly made you want to get up and move.

As she dried the plates behind the counter, she found her feet tapping to the rhythm, her body moving. Looking up, she saw that the customers at the table directly in front of her were jiggling their shoulders. The pair of students by the window who, if she recalled correctly were in a band that used African percussion instruments, started drumming on the table. The student next to them began clapping on the offbeats.

As the owner watched wide-eyed, the students' movements grew more pronounced, and after a while they stood up and started to dance. Sucked into their momentum, the people at the table in front of them also stood up. Then the one next to them.

The customers danced in the narrow gaps between the tables, each in their own unique way. The owner guessed that this wasn't how you were supposed to dance to Kawachi Ondo, but the music flowing from the speakers made their separate movements take on a wonderful rolling motion that seemed to express a single consciousness. The cafe was buzzing.

This, the young owner thought to herself, this is what I've been wanting to do. 🐵

© TOOGL

Stuart Dybek

———

Swifts, Swallows

THE GIRL'S BARE LEGS dangle over the ledge as she chats up a pigeon, although her intention, when she crawled out onto the tile roof of the Academy of Music, was to commune with the green-winged gargoyle. She'd like to learn his name. If it's a secret, it is one she would keep.

"Is that thunder?" her mother asks. The question carries from the window that has swung open beside the grand piano, which overlooks the rooftops of the city.

It is answered by a thundery glissando from the piano.

The girl knows that the eruption of notes isn't a passage from the nocturne her mother has been rehearsing. It's her mother's old piano teacher cutting in with his habit of running his hand down keyboards, across stringed instruments, or along the spines of women as if they'll ring out, too.

"There's nothing worse than the dog days of summer for keeping a Steinway in tune," the teacher complains. Or proclaims. His voice is an ongoing lecture. He said that gargoyles were fallen angels. The girl has dubbed him Professor KIA. His hand rushing along the keys reverberates through her body, making her seat on the ledge feel precarious. She avoids looking down at the cobblestone street just as she avoided looking out at the waves from the ship that she and her mother took to Europe. Instead of turning toward their voices coming from the open window, the girl holds her breath and stares across the city. If they should look out, she will pretend she hasn't heard them. Perhaps they *are* looking out and pretending they don't see her, so as not to reward her for always seeking attention.

"Mama's been communing with Chopin again," she tells the pigeon. "She wants to give me piano lessons for my birthday just like she got when she was nine, as if having to practice for hours every day is a present. Mama wanted her lessons because she fell in love with Chopin when she heard the Raindrop Prelude. Nana told her she could have lessons, but that girls her age weren't ready for Chopin. But after a few lessons, Mama's piano teacher, with his blond General Custer mustachios, informed Nana that Mama *was* ready for Chopin. She was precocious, he told Nana. And Nana said, *Do tell*—that should have been immediately obvious given that precociousness runs in the women of our family."

At the mention of Chopin, the pigeon begins to pace. Its iridescent head bobs in time to its back-and-forth along the ledge. Rather than being calming, its cooing sounds anxious.

"When I was a little girl," the girl says, and pauses, but neither the pigeon nor the gargoyle ask: *And what, pray tell, are you now?*

"When I was a little girl, the gift I begged my mother for was a pink clear-plastic umbrella so I could watch pink rain turn the world pink. Instead, I get piano lessons."

At the mention of the pink umbrella, a sooty cloud with smoldering edges rumbles over the roofs, trailing a gust that sucks the white curtains out of the windows of the Academy. The curtains flutter like the hankies waving farewell from the ocean liner that her mother insisted they sail to Europe on, so that once in their goddamn lives they could live like people did in a past when travel was elegant, and crossing an ocean took time enough for a cliché like "changing one's life" to mean something. What it meant, the girl thinks, was learning that once in her goddamn life was more than enough to be seasick for days.

She hears her name fluttering windblown from room to room as the windows of the Academy bang shut. In the silence that follows, she wonders if the windows have all been latched, and how hard the heel of a PF Flyer has to hammer to break a pane of beveled glass. She hears her name called again, this time from the echoey cobblestones on the narrow street.

Izabella! Izabella! Izabella!

The calling voices veiled in vapory mist sound as if the adults are playing a game of hide and seek. The street changes colors before the roof tiles do. The slick cobblestones show their true hidden shades the way the pebbles did at the beach in Brittany where the water was too cold and dangerous to swim because of an undertow.

"In Brittany, the beaches are pebbles, not sand, and you can find beautiful stones—marble, quartz, sea glass," she tells the pigeon. "Except by the time you get them home, they're dull, and you can't imagine why you wanted to keep them. They come back to life if you lick them, but once the spit dries, they're duller than ever."

The pigeon stops its pacing and cooing to listen.

"Once when Papa still lived at home, I snuck out like this and sat at the top of the stairs as if I was invisible and listened to him tell stories after a party for his birthday. I loved his stories. They made him seem like an exciting stranger," she says, and the pigeon appraises her, first through one pearly eye and then the other, as if looking through a monocle.

"His friends said he told a story like it was an aria. He listened to opera every Sunday. Opera was his church, he said. Once, when I was too little, he took me to an opera because it was a fairy tale about a Chinese princess, but I fell asleep. For his birthday cake, he insisted on a *baba au rhum.* The whole house smelled of rum. Instead of birthday candles Mama lit the giant candelabra on the sill of the picture window, and the candle flames reflected in the glass like there was a matching candelabra outside. People sang 'Happy Birthday,' and Papa blew out the candles from both candelabras, and the room got dark except for the streetlights shining in. Everyone was drunk from rum cake and champagne toasts, and no one knew I was hearing the story Papa was telling about how on his twenty-sixth birthday he was waiting at a train station in Ann Arbor for Mama. She was engaged then to the blond-mustachioed professor who'd been her piano teacher since she was nine, when he would French-kiss her if she had a good lesson. But there she was, Papa said, with the engagement ring that had belonged to the teacher's mother wrapped in a Kleenex she'd stuffed in her makeup case, riding a late-running train to their rendezvous. Papa sat on a bench beside the tracks and took out his sketchbook and a blue pencil and began to draw Mama from memory as clearly as if she were standing on the platform, modeling for him like in a figure drawing class. Not that she *had* modeled for him yet, he said. That would come later. It was as though the blue pencil, with a mind of its own, was drawing her playing a flute, Papa said, and he was grateful for that because his mind was off listening for her train, like a dog listening for its master's whistle. When he first sat down, Papa had noticed a bearded man with dirty, unclipped nails and a shock of gray hair that made him look like a grown-up Struwwelpeter from a scary German bedtime story sitting at the other end of the bench, eating popcorn they sold in the station from a greasy white bag. The man looked more like a hobo than a passenger, and Papa wondered if he'd scrounged the popcorn from the trash and was careful not to stare. Once the blue pencil began to draw, Papa forgot the man was there. But just when Papa thought he heard a sound like a far-off train whistle coming from the flute, the man asked, 'What are you looking at, you dumbass wobblehead?' 'Beg your pardon?' Papa said, afraid that the man thought Papa was sketching him because he looked like an escapee from an old fairy tale. 'I was not addressing you, sir, I am talking to *him*,' the man said, and pointed to a pigeon waiting for a popcorn handout."

A charged crackle, directly overhead, flashes like an exclamation point timed to punctuate the end of the story the girl has been telling. Both pigeons, the one at the train station and the one beside her on the ledge, simultaneously flap off as if offended. Before she can feel abandoned, a second flash sears through the underbelly of the clouds, releasing a flight of birds that swoop and orbit the roof of the Academy. Their wings glint metallic blue-green; their chittering is a single song. She saw similar birds in Brittany, skimming out of the glare over waves and sweeping across the pebble beach in pursuit of an invisible insect swarm.

"What are they?" she asked.

"I've never learned to tell swifts from swallows," her mother said. "But what does it matter, if we can watch them fly, as though we have ringside seats at a World War I dogfight?"

Unlike in Brittany, the birds above the Academy wheel near enough for her to feel as well as hear their whirr. The gargoyle must feel the vibrations, too, as the birds dart around him, streaking through gaps between the swollen raindrops splattering off his shoulders and back. He's hunched at a corner of the roof's edge, all but ready to spread his verdigris wings and launch into a glide over the wet sheen of the city.

The girl wishes she had an umbrella to unfold like wings. It needn't be pink. She can sense the gargoyle trying to commune with her, urging her to climb onto his back and hold tight to his horns. The invitation can only be passed between them as a thought, one that fills the mind. With his fixed, gaping shout of a mouth, should the gargoyle dare to speak, even a friendly word would roar. It would be like the thunder trying to utter a phrase that didn't shake the city. There's no letup in the whirring, rising pitch of the birds' insistent chitter, and when the gargoyle resists flapping off and following them in flight, the birds amaze her by diving into his roar of a mouth, and down his throat, perhaps to where his name is hidden.

Even dreams have not allowed her to feel so connected to her wildness within. Her amazement reassures her that she was right, when Mama sat at the Steinway, French-kissing her now white-mustachioed teacher, to sneak out a window. This downpour—part cloud, part rain, part birds—is her confirmation. Her reward. Had she stayed inside the Academy, she would not have seen how one by one the birds that vanished into the gaping mouth are spit back out, still part of the song, as if the gargoyle can sing what it has consumed back to life.

A melody that's remained forgotten despite attempts to reclaim it returns to her as if she is communing not with the gargoyle, but with the winter night when her father took her to the opera. She had fallen asleep against him, and he gently woke her, put his finger against her lips, and whispered in her ear that the Prince was singing "None Shall Sleep."

None shall sleep, her father whispers, *Listen.*

And when the Prince finished singing the aria whose words she didn't need to know, the ring of his voice left behind a silence that seemed like the world had gone to sleep. Then, someone shouted *Bravo!* And everyone was cheering, clapping, standing, stamping, *Bravo!* and Papa held her up above the audience in a way that felt like his *Bravo,* and beyond the orchestra and conductor, she could see the Prince standing alone on stage staring back at all of them while a great curtain of stars drew closed behind him.

Her arms extended for balance, her palms catching rain, the girl carefully stands on the ledge like she's directing the birds flying around her. *Bravo!* she thinks. It's not necessary to shout. When she rests her palm on the gargoyle, she feels him exhale. She doesn't need

© Satoshi Kitamura

Midori Osaki

Cricket Girl

translated by Asa Yoneda
and David Boyd

© TOOGL

NOT MANY WOULD know the heroine of our story, even if we were to mention her by name. For she was a person of few friendships, and led what might be called—in various senses—an elusive life. No doubt we could find many explanations for this if we looked into it, but for the purposes of our story, that would be a rather futile endeavor. Still, the winds of gossip have brought us a whisper or two. As one wind would have it, at the time that our heroine was born, the gods in charge of apportioning friendliness and sociability might have had a slight slip of the spoon. Or, she just so happened to be born at the unlucky hour when these gods were adream in their afternoon slumbers. Also, this slightly pedantic wind asserted, a certain school of thought called something-or-other-ism enjoyed a passing popularity in those days. A snippet of this thinking could have wound up in some corner of our heroine's head—or maybe her heart. As for this doctrine (the talkative wind continued), some say it was a very peaceful one, while others claim it was extremely raucous. Far be it for mere breezes like us to grasp the truth of what goes on in the land of the gods, so let us leave this particular question with the gods themselves. The influence of a tranquil philosophy might have been why this heroine of ours came to avoid loud places, such as those frequented by crowds of people; or maybe the heavenly fad was in fact so loud it had left her deafened. The hard-of-hearing are (our argumentative visitor raised their voice as they moved to conclude) naturally low in social inclination! They slip easily into misanthropic habits! They are avoidants!

The assertions of this windy visitor left us feeling that we understood only half the story. As for the rest, let's follow their lead and leave it to the mists enshrouding the land of the gods. So, we thought, albeit a little uncertainly, the heroine of this story must be one serious hermit. And if so, we'll have to handle her with a great deal of care. Let's follow her from the shadows, without making a sound, so she doesn't slip through our fingers.

We've muddied the beginning of our tale with insubstantial rumors, but we've heard still other whispers—to do with drugs. From what we've heard, the heroine of our story is a habitual user of a brownish powder. On the color of this substance there are competing theories, and we are unsure which to believe. Some say it isn't in fact brown but yellow; others say it takes the form of fine white crystals. Some say the amber color is actually the color of the bottle, meaning it must be a very potent drug indeed; others say what's yellow isn't the nostrum itself but the edible paper packets it comes in. At any rate, there's naught we can do but leave such matters to the god of trivial details. As mortal children of this earth, we simply pray for the continued sensitivity of the god in charge of things like medicinal coloring, and for their every sensory organ to function with the utmost fullness.

Whatever the substance's color, our heroine was a regular user of this medication. That much is beyond dispute. Yet it seems we can make no reliable reports as to its exact effects. Moments ago, we mentioned that the heroine of our story might have been deafened by the din of the discourse around her. Some say she turned to the powder to rescue herself from the melancholy of this silence; others say she continued to use it just to make herself all the deafer. Whichever the case, it was a psychoplegic, and doubtless a substance of the most pernicious variety—a drug that no one of sound character or well-rounded sensibility ought to put in their mouth.

We've also heard a handful of whispers about this mysterious powder's side effects. It acts on the gray matter of the cerebellum, the capillaries, and so on, making the sun too bright and crowds extremely unpleasant. Eventually, its users grow more and more averse to leaving the house during the day. Around the time that the sun vanishes beyond the earth's horizon, they finally regain their human faculties and venture out of their rented rooms. (Habitués of these substances generally seem to reside in such quarters.) And when it comes to where they go once they exit their hideaways, we hear the most sordid accounts. Apparently, those addicted set their hearts on that which is far away, grasping for what is out of reach rather than taking hold of what fills the air around them. They begin to fear, pull away from, and eventually disdain the living moving world outside their door based on their own solipsistic assumptions;

they come to feel more at home in the worlds they find on the screen at the movie theater, or atop a desk at the library. Of course this is all the drug's fault. On first hearing about the evils of this substance, we heaved the deepest sigh and muttered to ourselves: This stuff can be nothing other than an invention of the devil. To be born into the human world only to pull away from or even disdain those around you is an insult and a waste. If these addicts refuse to give up this wicked product, then surely a giant whip will grow out of the middle of the earth and strike at their beating hearts. We must do whatever it takes to save at least the heroine of our story from her devotion to this drug.

But despite these intentions, we did not cross paths with our heroine for some time. Just recently, however, we discovered that she's started to spend her time at the library, as if possessed of some great ambition.

WE SEEM TO have spent considerable time recounting tangential hearsay, to no particular end. Yet our readers need not conclude from these tales that the heroine of our story is a decadent woman. After all, these stories are only passing whispers. Let us now return our tale to the beginning. Suffice it to say— for a number of reasons, our heroine was a creature whose name is of no importance here.

THE MONTH IS MAY. A misty clutch of paulownia flowers had appeared on the trees at the edge of the field, and when it rained their scent echoed all the way into cricket girl's abode. She lived on the second floor in a rented room around ten feet square. The boards of the walkway that lay outside her sliding door were old and worn, so that no matter how carefully she stepped on them they would cry: *kew, kew, kew.*

Fortunately, it was going to be a rainy day, and the sun wasn't too bright either, so cricket girl decided to go to the library in the afternoon. She'd gotten ready to leave almost an hour ago, but as she contemplated the movements of the clouds, our cricket girl had found herself drifting off, so she stretched out her legs, made a stack of magazines into a pillow to rest her head, and took an hour-long nap. Then, when she woke up, she was greeted by the welcome sound of rain, and the scent of paulownia flowers hovered around her,

pale and a little faded in comparison to just a few days prior. All that was left for her to do was to throw on her jacket. Cricket girl's jacket was not that new, and just as worn out as the tired paulownia flowers. In her left pocket, a small handbag, even more venerable than the jacket. From her right pocket peeked the corner of a sheet of thick paper folded into fourths. This was the measure of cricket girl's outfit, which could not be described as too sharp or fresh. And in this ensemble, the girl herself looked, to our eyes, exactly as fresh as the jacket she was wearing.

Into the rainy field. The paulownia smell snuck in and filled the space under her umbrella. There was nothing she could do about it; lately, in this field, the smell was everywhere. But cricket girl didn't seem too enamored of the air here. From the depths of her nostrils, she snorted out a couple of impatient puffs of air, returning them to the atmosphere. Until she got out of this field, however, she couldn't get away from the smell of tired paulownia flowers; instinctively, she brought the handbag from her left pocket up to her face as she snorted again, then again.

Let's jump in to explain a little about why cricket girl was trying to avoid the smell of these flowers while crossing this field in the rain. As far as we can tell, it's extremely impudent to reject the fragrance of such a flower as the paulownia, which has captured the pens of so many sentimentalist poets over the years. Notwithstanding, the scent that draped around her was worn out, almost finished, inarguably neurotic... And cricket girl, as a result of her overindulgence in that devilish remedy, had lately come down with a moderate case of neurosis herself.

To make a slight digression in our story, we once knew a medic named Tōhachi Kōda who worked at a hospital known for treating cases of schizo-psychology. This was a man who, in the past, had committed not a few sacrileges against the god of all that is cloaked in mystery. For example, out of an excess of enthusiasm for schizo-psychological research, he set out on a tour with nothing but an armful of collected plays and a notebook; then, on reaching his first destination, he instructed a young girl to read aloud passionate scenes from romantic plays and took notes on the effects this had on her enunciation and emotional state. We have a handful of favorite episodes about Tōhachi's notes, but putting these aside for another day, we would like to cast our minds on an idea that he stumbled upon during that trip, in order to explicate cricket girl's state of mind as she walked through the rain aiming for the library.

A fine drizzle over the spring field. The scent of paulownia flowers that have grown weary of the season. Two or three minutes after leaving her room, cricket girl's faded spring jacket was already thoroughly dampened. The sight of someone's back as they walk away can evidently put a damper on the viewer's spirit, for we couldn't help but let out a sigh at the scene in this May field. Cricket girl's appearance could not be said to be very fitting of the spring landscape. The piece of clothing shrouding her figure as we observed her from behind was, if technically a spring jacket, faded to a color worthy of an autumn garment. It made us want to pluck her image out of that scene and place it instead within an autumn wind.

Now, Tōhachi's theory went something like this: When the equilibrium of a person's nervous system is disturbed, through the unfortunate effects of pharmaceuticals, or mental stress, et cetera, this person will make sustained efforts to hide away from anything fierce, such as the summer sun. At the same time, they will also start to reject that which is feeble, like the scent of flowers that are about to fall. This is a psychological need arising from the patient's physical state, and assuredly not a case of wishful thinking on the part of we schizo-psychologists! Should the patient have to leave their house during the time of year when the sun's rays are strong, they will delay their daytime errands until after dark, or hole up in their room with their blinds drawn and wait days for a rainy respite. And when they need pass under, for instance, a paulownia in late spring, they will snort repeatedly, using rapid nasal exhalations to prevent the scent of neurotic paulownias from entering their body. In short, the nervously ill will avoid the nervously ill. They do this to protect themselves from experiencing sympathy for a fellow sufferer, for both they and the flowers, while one human and one botanic, are equally prey to nervous disorders, and therefore share a kinship, &c, &c.

We may have distorted Tōhachi Kōda's hypothesis somewhat, due to the nebulousness of our own memory, but in effect, this was the mental state that led cricket girl to go to great lengths to avoid inhaling the smell of the paulownia blooms. Having made her way past them, she reached the bus stop and caught her ride to the library.

LISTEN CLOSELY—we're about to let you in on a secret. Under the spell of the devil's powder, the heroine of our story had fallen in love. How shall we describe the beginnings of this flame burning inside her? It was a rather roundabout affair.

One day, cricket girl happened to stumble upon a story that began with a quaint and familiar-sounding line: "Long ago, there lived a man and a woman who lived entirely for each other, and nothing could come between them."

It went on to describe the romance of an unusual poet; his name was William Sharp, and through the inexplicable workings of his heart, he had fallen for a female poet of the time named Fiona Macleod. Theirs was a tender, intimate bond—more so than any love the world has ever known. The two exchanged heartfelt love letters, even poetry. We can imagine that, cast into the conventions of our country, their poems might have sounded something like these:

*kimi ni yori omohinarahinu yo no naka no
hito ha kore wo ya kohi to ifuramu*

*narahaneba yo no hito goto ni nani wo kamo
kohi to ha ifu to tohishi ware shi mo*

And yet at the very heart of this affair was a mystery: not a soul in the world had ever laid eyes upon Miss Macleod. She was therefore to her contemporaries a most ethereal poet. They knew her to be hidden away somewhere beyond the reach of the world, where she wrote pale poems with a cosmic bent. From time to time, she would visit her beloved Mr. Sharp for a period of several days. But what did she do while she was there? She was a mystic poet who spent all her time writing, never appearing in the public eye. And so it was that on occasion members of Mr. Sharp's social circle would remonstrate with him. As they were not the sort to stand for poets of this earth to be so ethereal, they harangued: "We hear that Miss Fiona Macleod is a poet of remarkable radiance and beauty. In which case, sir, you do us a tremendous disservice. You have not once arranged for us to meet her. Today we intend to set our eyes on her person, and we are prepared to wait, however many hours it may take, until our desire is fulfilled."

At this, a dark shadow fell over Mr. William Sharp's brow. Without even looking his friends in the eye, he began to mutter, apparently unaware of what he himself was saying. He rustled on in fits and starts, like a banana palm in late fall: "Oh, I'm afraid that's a formidable request. She's already left on a journey somewhere far away. She's no longer by my side. It was last evening—oh, my mind is in the clouds for some reason. I'm losing track of time, the passage of time, and yet I'm fairly certain the sky I can see in my mind is that of last night. It was the two of us, Fiona and I, lying there, as close as could be, gazing up at the stars in the heavens. At some remove, the planets . . ."

"Sharp!" his friends interjected. "What we want to hear from you is much more earthly. We are no astronomers. The stars? The planets? Great heavens! How long do you intend to keep us in the dark? This is why they say that people in love are irresponsible and can't be trusted. You enter into the tale of your conquest only to veer suddenly into the night sky. Sharp! The two of you were as close as could be, and then . . . ?"

Such company will never be satisfied until one speaks of kissing and the bedroom. With a sigh, William Sharp answered:

"We kissed, of course. And yet between the two of us what is a kiss? Oh, as I gazed upon the planets, my Fiona slipped out of my heart, and I know not where she has gone . . ."

"Come now, enough of your swizzle. Bring us a snifter of fizzy lemon soda and a persimmon-lacquered fan—the type used to stoke the coals of those Oriental braziers. The bigger the better. We've heard they have an autumnal mien that will help to cool any ears subjected to your lovesick twaddle."

Sharp remained silent. His visitors went on insisting that he introduce them to Miss Macleod. Our noses, they claimed, are particularly sensitive to the scent of beauties! She can't be more than ten feet away as we speak! Ah, this fragrance! Miss Macleod must be in the next room consoling herself at her dressing table! This is, yes, that famous perfume known throughout history—ever since the age of King Tut! When combined with the smell of a beautiful woman's skin, it's simply irresistible to dandies like us! Mr. Sharp! Go and fetch your guest from her dressing room at once! they cried. Sharp remained silent.

So did William Sharp and Fiona Macleod spend many long years together. During that time, the world never managed to catch so much as a glimpse of Miss Macleod. Then, finally, several months after Sharp's demise, it was discovered that Macleod had also been summoned by the god of eternity—at the same hour on the same day as Sharp. Furthermore, she had passed in the very same bed, of the very same affliction. And yet only one body was visible to those who looked upon them: the body of William Sharp.

Now we'd better return to cricket girl, our heroine who was reading this well-worn tale. As she got deeper into the piece, she felt an autumn wind sweep through her. This was the feeling that swept through cricket girl whenever something struck her soul. (We're not entirely certain whether this was a psychological effect, or some sort of physical sensation.) And once that autumn wind had passed, cricket girl was in love. The object of her affection would be the thing, event, or person that had sent that wind through her.

Through some strange detour of the mind, we seem to have greatly expanded the territory of this thing called love. At any rate, this was how our heroine fell for a poet from another land.

We've jumped around a bit, but the tale ends as follows: two souls vanished from this world leaving behind but a single body. It was a death of a most unusual nature. But how was anyone to know what exactly had transpired there? They held a funeral for Wm. Sharp, a man born to this earth who gave his heart to the heavens. (Much the same as his dear Fiona Macleod, he was a mystic who dedicated his poetic spirit to the ambling of the sun and the frolicking of the planets.) Yet as Sharp was returned to the soil, several of his friends wondered, "Where in this world does Miss Macleod mourn William's death?" And during the funeral procession, these gentlemen—whose waist pockets were always stuffed with more French ham than they could contain—grew all the fatter, thinking loudly and unabashedly to themselves: Alas, poor Sharp, who was always muttering away about clouds and mists, has finally departed this plane! That pale, wan soul . . . he must be feeling as though he's returned home! The moon and the stars and the progress of the sun, and the endless, the eternal, the infinite, the Unknown Goal! Great heavens! The man spoke of nothing of substance! No wonder his soul now travels the unending sky together with the wind! It's no more than he deserves! Speaking of which—when this procession arrives at its destination, we're supposed to offer up a eulogy to Sharp's soul on behalf of all us heavy-set gentlemen! How ironic! It won't be long now until we arrive! Time to face the music! To dampen our booming voices ever so slightly and say:

> To all the gentlemen and ladies gathered here
>   to bid a dear friend farewell!
> Mr. William Sharp was
>   a most vaporous poet!
> During his esteemed life, he penned three books
>   of poetry—
>   or perhaps it was seven—
> All full of noble ideas
>   expressed entirely in the form of abstract
>   nouns!

Okay! Now for Fiona Macleod! Yes, Miss Macleod! On account of Sharp's stinginess, we never once had the chance to lay eyes upon her brow! That weaselly Sharp, always coming up with excuses to keep her away from us, right up to the end—truly, his jealousy knew no bounds! Fiona! I can see you now—set free from his possessiveness, having a carefree yawn somewhere far from here! A woman who has just lost her beloved will enjoy a meal the very next day! This is an eternal axiom derived from our experiences with one thousand women! Even as their eyes fill with tears, their mouths are already occupied with some new dish of food! Oh, but where is our Miss Macleod awaiting her next plate? Ah, our noses once again detect that perfume of the Pharaohs! We will find her, even if it means parting every tussock in every last field! Then! We'll need to pick out a scent to strew about the bed! Because each woman's skin has a unique scent all its own! Ah! Thanks to Sharp's misguided jealousy, we have yet to be introduced to the scent of her skin! How I doubt there could be another man so jealous in all the world! We will do anything to find her—search high and low, through field after field! In her poetry, she is just as liable as our late Sharp to wax on and on about clouds and mists, but I suspect that, should we search high and low and winkle her out, she just might turn out to be possessed of a surprising body! From what we hear, unlike her poetry, some of the love letters she's written to Sharp are rather corporeal! As it should be, quite as it should be! I'm willing to wager our Miss Macleod is no willow-waisted woman of the mists! There's a strange new facility somewhere in the Orient! According to the findings of one of its doctors, a man by the name of T. Kohda, it's willowy women who write voluptuous poems and full-figured women who write wispy ones! What a splendid theory! If so, it's all the more urgent that we search high and low for the body of Fiona Macleod!

Thus the quiet procession wended its way toward its eventual destination, with all these different ideas in tow. But when it came to Fiona Macleod's whereabouts, Sharp's old friends weren't even close to the truth. For unbeknownst to them, Macleod was at that very moment lying within the body of William Sharp—just as dead as he, though there was no corpse—secretly receiving the self-same obsequies. Fiona Macleod truly was a poet of the clouds: the product of a split within the psyche of William Sharp, a woman with no physical form. So it was that when her dear Sharp departed this world, she went with him. And yet the letters exchanged between the two were as real as could be. When this poet of multiple minds was a man, he picked up Sharp's pen and wrote letters to his beloved Macleod, and when he became a woman, she took up Macleod's pen and wrote to her beloved Sharp. At some later time, a physician of the psyche may read these letters and pick apart Sharp's soul, calling this a case of *doppelgängerism* or something equally recondite. Neither can we rule out the possibility of a certain ephemeral poet, writing in an attic in the Orient, taking this crystalline poetess of a distant land as the subject of her scribblings for her own intangible artistic ends. Psychologists and writers are blasphemers in every age . . . They do nothing but pollute the godly domains of Eros and the Muses. The more they meddle, the more they destroy the mystic world in which souls such as Sharp make their home.

This was the end of the old story that cricket girl had found.

THE LIBRARY STOOD at the top of the hill, a little closer to the open sky than the town. On this day, it was awash in gray. To cricket girl, the building's facade was as moody as an excitable turkey. When the sun shone, it was an aloof, shining ivory tower; in the rain, it turned a companionable dun. A rain-darkened gray deals even a drug-addled head only the gentlest of blows.

However, within the library's walls, the shadow of William Sharp, the poet who had stolen cricket girl's heart, remained elusive. Cricket girl's notes were far from copious, despite days of research. Wallowing in her despair, she sketched corners of the different clouds that visited her mind in the empty spaces of her notebook, or paused in her perusal of voluminous literary histories—her unhappy discovery was that the thicker the book, the less its writer had to say about the poet on whom her heart was set—to ruminate on the dubious tastes of their compilers, killing time in a way that was as mute and unproductive as a plant. Her doing this benefited not a single living soul on the face of the earth.

Cricket girl's notes on William Sharp were, for the aforementioned reason, woefully lacking. Finally, after combing through who knows how many volumes, she found a preface that only piqued her misery:

"Now, the last thing I have to say is that the owner of this publishing house has some lofty ideals. He made it clear to me that he absolutely refuses to print so much as a line of any literature that he considers insalubrious, mentally ill, etc. That being the case, I had no choice but to nix a handful of poets I'd already included in my manuscript whom he would have outright despised. The least I can do is mention them here. In no particular order: three members of the Roseaux Pensants, several of the Yellow Sensitivists, and all of the Late Cocaine School; Oscar Wilde for his immoral activities, and William Sharp for confusing the world by taking every available opportunity to turn himself into a woman."

What good was such a note to cricket girl? All it did was make her headache worse. We understand that when human beings feel sad or disappointed, their usual illnesses and ailments weigh on them even more heavily. For this reason, our heroine had to stagger out of the reading room and seek refuge in the muted atmosphere of the basement.

Down the narrow stone steps and into the flagstone hallway. To the right was a short row of stalls. Turning left, she went into the women's lunchroom. It was always quiet there outside of mealtimes, with a dim air that lay undisturbed. It also had a great kettle of hot water she could use to take her medicine. The water steamed out of the spout and into her cup. Holding it up against the weak light from the window, she saw the water had a grayish tint. Then cricket girl got the powder out of her shabby bag and took a dose. Anyone could have seen her do it. The air in the room was really very tired. And the courtyard beyond the glass was full of misty May drizzle. Conditions like these usually inspire people to start singing at the top of their lungs, or talk to someone, or find a bit of bread to keep their mouths busy. The heroine of our story knew all about this kind of human behavior from her time living in rented rooms. So she got the idea that she could at least try eating a little bread. Just then, from the other side of the lunchroom, she heard the sound of a pencil being sharpened. Someone had been there the whole time, sitting in the gloomiest corner of the room. Immediately, and beyond a single doubt, cricket girl got it into her head that the person was a memorizer of midwifery. A most convenient conversation partner. But this person kept her face buried in her books as though she had blinders on, showing no indication of being open to an overture from cricket girl. Not only had cricket girl been completely unaware of the other woman until that moment, the other woman remained ignorant of cricket girl's presence even now. How could this be? Cricket girl gave up and walked over to the bakery.

"Donut twist."

The unfriendly sounds tumbled out of her mouth, which had fallen out of the habit of making conversation. The girl behind the counter raised her head and looked at cricket girl with a hint of exasperation before handing her a paper bag containing the donut.

Regarding the color of cricket girl's heart during the time it took her to eat the first half of her donut twist there is little to report. She had nothing on her mind but the donut. She even seemed to have forgotten all about the terrible blow she'd been dealt by the preface she'd just read. Halfway through her donut she slowed down considerably. Listlessly licking at the chocolate creme, she opened a voiceless conversation with the person in the opposite corner of the lunchroom.

"Excuse me . . . is midwifery as demanding as they say?"

The woman, however, remained hunched over her memorizing, moving not so much as a muscle.

Cricket girl directed one last attempt at silent conversation toward the shadowed brow of her counterpart three tables over. "Keep it up, widow (cricket girl couldn't think of any other way to address this thin, dark figure)—I hope you'll be a full-fledged midwife come autumn. And may you tread on dawn crickets every morning as your clinic prospers. If I spoke to you now of crickets, I'm sure you'd only laugh. But I'd like to whisper a confession to you: I can't get crickets off my mind. It fills my head with useless thoughts day in and day out. But even thoughts like these take bread. Which means I have to alarm my dear mother with telegrams no matter the season. Letters and postcards are more than I can bear to face. My mother lives in the country. Widow, do you have a mother, too? Oh, I hope she lives to be a hundred! But widow, the world has never been kind to mothers. When a daughter's mind is troubled, her mother's heart is stricken many times worse. Ah, Fiona Macleod! When you lived as a woman poet, did you ever want to ask the scientists this—how somebody might live on nothing but mist? That's what I want more than anything.

I just get so tired of always having to ask for bread, bread, bread . . ."

The sun was setting on the library basement. 🐒

Note from the translators: Two poems appear on page 123. For the purposes of this story, one translation of the first poem, which was composed by the Heian aristocrat Ariwara no Narihira, might be translated as "From you I've finally learned / what it is the world calls love." The response, from his dear friend Ki no Aritsune, could be translated as "I know nothing of this world, let alone love / should you not be the one to show me!"

What kind of old person would you like to be?

Responses from eight poets

© Lauren Tamaki

JUST LIKE HER
Mimi Hachikai
translated by Lisa Hofmann-Kuroda

There are few people I can recall
Wanting to be like
In my memory,
Facing the autumn wind

    Like that old lady, for example
    Yes, that old lady who sold vegetables

When I was a child
She'd show up at our door sometimes
With a towel on her head, a basket on her back
When I looked in,
A few meager crops from the field
Lined the inside like a soliloquy—

Will I be able to make things grow
In the field of poetry?
Will I be allowed to?
Carrying a basket on my back
With the fruits of my meager harvest,
Will I walk on as the seasons change?

    Like that old lady, for example
    And my best friend's piano teacher, that's right—
    Not my own

Who insisted on living alone
Without children
Always doing everything herself
Alone even when she fell
The sound of the piano
Following the rain like a soliloquy—

Will I be able to perform
The piano music of a poem?
Will I be allowed to?
Even when these familiar melodies
Are on the verge of leaving me
Will I be able to play on, calmly,
As the seasons change?

RAIN CLOUDS
Hirata Toshiko
translated by Chris Corker

Rather than boat across the Sanzu River,
to reach the Underworld, I'd rather swim.
That way I could greet all the freighters,
listening to the seagulls cry.
Having already died,
there's little to fear from drowning,
but with fitness being a factor,
the quicker I make it, the better.

People fret about growing old
and live lives weighed down by that anxiety,
even though there is no guarantee of age,
even though this day may be their last.
Death is random.
All ages welcome.

All the people we wished to see but could not meet.
All the places we wished to go but could not reach.
Not only failing to become who we wanted to be,
but becoming old without ever trying.

The sweet grandma does not please me,
and being an old crone does not come easy.
To be neither sweet nor a witch,
neither here nor there—
that is what I am.

The old lady from my neighborhood
when I was a child,
always gazing out from the upstairs window.
Maybe she was watching
for death to roll in on the rain clouds.

Just like that lady from long ago,
I will stare out from the upstairs window,
waiting for the rain clouds I know will come.
Waiting with fear,
with anticipation.

SOMEDAY, MY ANNIHILATION WILL COME
Iko Idogawa
translated by Lisa Hofmann-Kuroda

Someday, my annihilation will come.
The monkey rubs two halves of a stone together
with a stern look, he listens closely
to the sound of the flat, broken pieces.
His ears delight in it
though the white hair around them gets in the way.
In the crowd, children
try their hardest to feign ignorance
of what the adults are doing.
They walk two by two,
covering their ears from time to time.
On days when the sun is harsh, the adults
know which hill to climb to feel the wind's relief.

Someday, my annihilation will come.
The elephant's skin is dark, his back
is covered with grass.
His thin ears strike his shoulders, they do as they please.
They're scarred, and full of holes,
not wrinkled so much as wrapped in protective lines—
rocks, fossils, a large cracked earth
which clings to him.
His eyes are volcanoes that erupt with tears
filling the air with the scent of boiling water.
I haven't the slightest idea if his is a youthful cry.

Someday, my annihilation will come.
Do you think the waves will remember
their present shape?
My grandmother doesn't answer.
I should have leaned in closer to speak.
She chews on a thin but sinewy piece of meat
sucks on it then spits it out, unable to swallow it.
They used to scold me for doing that when I was a kid,
my grandmother laughs with an astonished look.
So I'd just swallow it whole.
Skillfully she releases the air in her lungs.
Her four limbs grow thin, shrink.
The chest that panted countless times swells
then sleeps. She's light, equipped with everything.

REACH OUT THOSE YOUNG LIMBS

Mizuki Misumi

translated by Chris Corker

Why do the stars shine?
Why does the rain fall?
And why, when the stuff inside has been eaten,
does the candy tin end up empty?

Not letting go of that little me
who never failed to ask *why*?

My days full of words
openly accepted,
lovingly collected,
eyed with suspicion.

Why?
Body alone continuing to grow,
pretending to be an adult,
but deep down the little me
yelling herself hoarse.

I never want to become
so sure when I'm older
that there is nothing more to learn,
convinced to abandon doubt.

In the end
I want to be the tree,
alone in the desert,
who, when a bird comes by,
will ask *why do you fly*?

I want to be the withering tree,
motionless and alone,
sensing and absorbing
the wonder of this universe.
Easily frightened by it,
saddened by it,
delighted by it.

ANT AS A GLASS OF WATER
Sawako Nakayasu

They ask and I say no because I figure they are unlikely to accept my
answer anyway but they insist on an answer so I say fine, I'll tell you.
I'll tell you that when I grow very old I would like to become a glass of
water. No no you must continue to be human. See, I told you I didn't
want to answer. No, please. You must continue to be human. But why.
Because you are one now. All the more in my old age I would like to
be a glass of water, I'd make such a nice glass of water, don't you think?
So useful, so desired. No no you cannot be a glass of water. Fine then
I'll be an ant. No you cannot be an ant. For the same reasons, I imagine.
Yes. Please. Do continue to be human. But why won't you even give
me a chance. In fact, screw that—I'll be an ant, and that ant will
be a glass of water. I do not understand what you mean. Here's what
you can do with my old age. Swirl it first, to release the aroma.
I am a well-tempered ant, a nicely adjusted glass of water. Breathe it
in, my molecules of ant scent. Tip it to the left, to the right, watch
the contents swish to the head, to the tail, and back again to the head.
Contemplate my black translucency, the sleek curve of exoskeleton
that fits nicely in your hand, and imagine how nourishing, this universal
elixir of ant. Daily, every day, forever, moreover. I am delighted to
age so beautifully into this ant, this glass of water. I am grateful.
I am joyful. I am overflowing with vigorous survival. Thank you, ant.
Thank you, water. Our relationship is both banal and extraordinary.
I am an ant. I am a glass of water. *Plus ça change.* Same as it ever was.
The question is no longer to drink or not to drink. The wind outside
is punishing, and yet look at you now, holding me so tenderly. I knew
it would be easier than you could ever know, to age so nicely into
this ant that is a glass of water. It is what it is, as they say into their
covered mouths.

I COOK, AND EAT
Sayaka Ōsaki

translated by Lisa Hofmann-Kuroda

Nothing has changed, you know, since I was twenty
But I do think I've gotten much better at cooking
Now I rely on my sense of smell to tell me
Yes—it's this one, this one is my life.
On the kitchen counter is a glass
Filled to the brim with chilled white wine.
I take a few sips here and there,
As I cook whatever I want,
But only as much as I can eat by myself.
Steamed cabbage with cumin.
Grated carrots and finely chopped cheese.
Noodle soup heaped with condiments.
Steamed chicken. Sauteed mushrooms. Salted egg.
Yogurt cake with rum.

There were these women I used to admire.
A woman who made and designed her own clothes.
A woman who ran a salon that attracted only men.
A woman who translated lots of children's literature.

One woman smoked cigarettes that made her look cool.
One woman traveled around and sang onstage.
One woman wrote and wrote and never fell in love.
Why did I admire them for things like that?
It's hard to explain. (And besides, those women aren't around anymore.)

I sauté some turnips in olive oil
Add some salt, and lemon juice, and eat.
The texture, the saltiness, the smell of the oil and lemon juice—
All of it brings back the memory of the feasts those women used to make me.

And then I think, you know, I guess I'm fine.
I've eaten my fill.
I can make it on my own now
(and this is my life, anyway)—
This day, filled with lovely smells.

FOR YOKO SENSEI
Shii
translated by Chris Corker

Right now it's quiet, almost silent.
Do you remember the day I wrote those words?
And do you recognize me across the table from you,
by the window of the antique café?

Voices raised late at night and a dazzle of light behind eyelids. What was it that you did then? Your face hidden in your hands as you turned slowly towards me, but the words that followed calm (*another person I care for gone*): Sensei, Yoko Sensei. We were both six that spring. Her class the first for us at school, but the last she would teach. We took turns filling in the classroom diary we shared, our entries concealed within origami hearts. And yet for all the many hearts you gave to me, there were always more to come. I am searching for the pages we used for just the two of us. Our secret correspondence. Mirrored in the glass of a worn-out kaleidoscope, the trials and tribulations of youth— the education received, knowledge acquired, the laughter and the hugs, the stories of ill-fated romances, and the smiles when our names were called at the beginning of class. "And who might you be?" asked with a puzzled look and that bitingly sweet tone. (*If you ever want to see me you can always call my name. Anytime, I'll be there.*) Back then and even now, decades later but still unsure of who I am, I remember being taken into your slender arms with care, the kiss on my young flushed cheeks and the repeated words, *I love you. . . I love you,* spoken as a single line of your tears dampened my cool face.

   Even if I were to lose all the memories we shared, those scant but precious three words would shine through the void, helping me every day as the years pass.

DEAD LOAD
Rob Winger

In order to carry traffic, the structure must have some weight, and on short
spans this dead load weight is usually less than the live loads. On longer
spans, however, the dead load is greater than live loads, and, as spans get
longer, it becomes important to design forms that minimize dead load.
—David P. Billington and Philip N. Billington, *Encyclopaedia Britannica*

Midafternoon, we're still riding
trains to offices, surprised
each season comes on quick,

that the kids, already, are some
new age, that your old friend's
positive X-rays mean the evening's

no longer far off. We've all got
debt loads. There are beaches
we'd like to reach, hallucinogens

we haven't tried, novels
left unopened. But almost
every bridge we're crossing

was shaped by the kind of falsework
this deck's dead load remembers best,
a frame at first held fast, suspended

by cables or floating beams or bolted
to prestressed towers, gothic
anchorage, sure abutment and pier.

The bridge deck, then, is a series
of decks, a sequence linked, your life,
into some semblance of a single story.

Mid-span, we look up at sunshine
or falling snow, down to covered plate
girders, I-beams, expansion joints.

Below us are rivers or chasms that only
our foundations touch, railroad tracks
leading elsewhere, other crossings.

To this specific midpoint observation platform,
the dusk is coming fast. The other side's right
there, waiting to release the span's live load.

What role, if any, does music play in your translation process? Remarks from nine translators

You would think that music could aid translation in so many ways. Translators might even develop a playlist for each author or for specific works. On the other hand, would it not be better to set music aside, so that its rhythms don't conflict with the rhythms fermenting in the translator's mind? Is that even possible, given that so many of us are afflicted by nagging earworms of one invasive species or another? In the following pages, nine translators respond to the question. Their answers might surprise you!

JEFFREY ANGLES
on musical alchemy

Classical music is one of my greatest passions, tied for first place with literature. Although I no longer perform, my love for music still burns so strongly that I listen to music nearly every moment I'm in my study. Music keeps me in the moment, carrying me through the long sedentary hours that translation requires. Without music, my patience grows short and my mind wanders. In fact, I suspect that it's thanks to music that I've translated as much as I have.

It's hard to describe the almost alchemical associations that guide my musical choices for a particular project. Avant-garde poetry from the 1970s or 1980s might inspire me to put on experimental music from the same decades, maybe György Ligeti's complex rhythms or Tōru Takemitsu's broad brushstrokes of orchestral color. Prose from the early twentieth century might lead me in a more modernist direction, perhaps the grand gestures of Samuel Barber or the quartets of Béla Bartók, whereas more strident, plot-driven prose goes well with Dmitri Shostakovich or Sergei Prokofiev.

Sometimes the associations are more direct. While finishing my translations of Shigeru Kayama's novels *Godzilla* and *Godzilla Raids Again,* I explored every nook and cranny of Akira Ifukube's oeuvre. Besides the soundtracks for the Godzilla films, Ifukube produced a vast body of work. Drawing upon the Ainu rhythms and Japanese folk melodies of his native Hokkaido, he wrote in a modernist idiom to produce some of the most driving, exciting orchestral music written in East Asia during the twentieth century.

Music does occasionally lead me astray. Recently, a friend proofreading my work pointed out that I had made an odd error, mistranslating the word for *akanbō* (baby) as "red dragonfly" (*aka-tombo*). The reason, I immediately realized, wasn't just the similar sound. I'd been playing a recording of Kōsaku Yamada's music, and even though it didn't include his setting of the Japanese folk song "Red Dragonfly," somehow the memory of that piece had found its way into my writing. Surprising how music can creep into one's subconscious!

POLLY BARTON
on translating in silence

My days of listening to music as I translate (or at least, translate anything that I care about, anything that isn't purely administrative) are over, I think, and I'd be lying if I said I didn't miss them. There was a time when I could have music on as I worked so long as it wasn't wordy—my preference was for contemporary classical like Steve Reich or Philip Glass, or else cheesy eighties New Age à la Mike Oldfield—but these days, as diva-ish as it might sound, I crave silence. In fact, I'll up my diva score by saying, in full earnestness, I can't listen to music because I need to listen to the words. Often when I'm asked to explain particular translation decisions I've made, I find myself at a loss. I always feel like appealing to "intuition" at those times is a cop-out, so the word I reach for instead is "rhythm," and as I say it, I'm unsure whether I'm telling the truth or not—whether I'm saying anything at all. But I think, on reflection, that I am. I need silence because I need to listen not just to what the words say but to how they sound, the pitch and the pace of them, and it's that which I'm trying to nail in English too. Possibly, that quest is the very thing that leads me to the most "creative" and "intuitive" deviations, the sorts of decisions that are hardest to justify in words. Possibly, next time I'm asked, I'll just hand my interlocutor a copy of *Music for 18 Musicians,* and walk away with a diva-ish shrug.

DAVID BOYD
on feeling it

I was a Japanese major when I finished college, but my original major was music.

When I translate, I find that some of the things I picked up in my music courses have been just as useful as anything I learned in Japanese class.

My first semester, I signed up for a jazz course that met in the auditorium. We had a great sound system, and we made the most of it. It was a big class—maybe two hundred students—and every meeting we'd listen to a handful of songs together.

On the day of our first class, the professor came in, gave us some very simple instructions, then put on a song. "Just move to the music," he said. "Be natural."

The song was "Could You Be Loved" by Bob Marley. He let it play for about a minute, then hit pause, looked right at me, and said: "You . . . What do you think you're doing?"

"Nothing," I said. And that's the truth. I was doing *nothing*.

"You think what you're doing is natural, that not moving is natural, but you're wrong. You're fighting against yourself. Your body wants to move. When you're listening to music, moving is natural."

He was right, of course. I was in my own head—and it was keeping me from feeling the music.

You can end up in your own head when you're translating, too. But feeling the text, responding to it, is the most natural thing in the world. When you're translating, the source text needs to move through you.

The only way to make sure the text gets where it needs to go is for you to move with it.

ANNA ELLIOTT
on creating another melody

I know that some people listen to music when translating, but I find it distracting, perhaps because as I translate I am listening for the melody of the original and trying to create another melody—or, if not a melody, at least a rhythm—in my translation. Often, the simpler the original sentence, the harder it is to do it that kind of musical justice.

Let's take the first sentence of Haruki Murakami's story "Tony Takitani" as an example. It reads, "トニー滝谷の本当の名前は、本当にトニー滝谷だった." In my opinion, this sentence has a wonderful rhythm and melody: it rises and falls, speeds up and slows down, pauses in the middle, and has a strong ending. Repetition is employed to great effect. The estranging effect of the reversed name order will be lost in translation, but can the musical quality of this sentence be preserved somehow?

In Jay Rubin's English translation we read, "Tony Takitani's real name was really that: Tony Takitani." We get a pause near the end, and we also get the repetition of "real" and "really," as well as of the name. But we also immediately notice that the "melody" is much shorter. Is there a way around it? Probably not. The words 本当のand 本当にhave five moras each, and I can't think of any five- or even four-syllable English words meaning "real" or "really."

When translating into Polish, I didn't have a problem with words being too short, but unfortunately, words meaning "real" and "really" are not similar enough to get the same effect of repetition. After much trial and error, I ended up with a sentence that reads something like, "Tony Takitani was really called Tony Takitani"—not only much shorter, but also much less melodious and playful than the original. An epic failure, musically speaking. Maybe I *should* have had music playing in the background . . .

TED GOOSSEN
on Dylan and translation

There were those who scoffed when Bob Dylan won the Nobel Prize for literature, but I was not one of them. I've been singing his songs all my life. His lyrics are a kind of reservoir that I can dip into as I try to wrest some sort of natural flow from this beautiful yet confounding language that, through a simple twist of fate, has become the focus of so much of my life.

But it isn't Dylan alone. There are so many other songs, hundreds of them, that I have picked up in the sixty-plus years that I have been singing and strumming. This can be both a blessing and a curse—why should "Itsy Bitsy Teenie Weenie Yellow Polkadot Bikini" keep popping up unbidden? When I was working on Haruki Murakami's first two novels, *Hear the Wind Sing* and *Pinball 1973,* the music in my head definitely helped. I didn't have to put "California Girls" on the stereo—I could already hear it.

Now that I am translating Hiromi Kawakami, though, influences from song lyrics follow a more circuitous route, and I often have to turn my damper down to block infelicitous phrases from blowing in on the wind. All it takes is a few lines of a song leaking up from the living room to completely throw me off my rhythm. Now even my grandchildren know not to play songs with lyrics, even nursery rhymes, when Papa is working.

Luckily, I can listen to Japanese songs without being distracted. And jazz and classical music too, since they are forms I know so little about. If I learned too much about those traditions, I'd probably have to turn them off as well. Roll over, Beethoven!

SACHIKO KISHIMOTO
on having a brain like a one-room apartment
translated by Margaret Mitsutani

If you'd asked me three years ago, I would have answered in three lines or so. "The role of music in my translation process? There isn't one, really. I mean, there's hardly any music in my life to begin with. I go out of my way to listen to music about twice a year, if that. And of course, it's always quiet while I'm translating."

Then came Spotify, and everything changed. That's a good song, I'll think, and when I search for it, the app comes back with "You might also like . . ." and then gives me several recommendations. I add the ones I like to my playlist, which keeps getting longer.

Then there's Shazam, which I use to find the titles of songs that catch my fancy while I'm in a restaurant or listening to the radio. It's amazing how I always get a hit on the first try. Thanks to this app, my playlist gets even longer. So now, music is always there for me when I need a break. I can't even imagine what it was like being me three years ago, when I only listened to music "about twice a year, if that."

But to get back to the original question, I'm afraid the answer is still "It's always quiet while I'm translating." Sorry, I think it's because my brain isn't built for multitasking. I can translate or listen to music, but not both at the same time. If I put something on while I'm working, my hands stop while I listen to the music.

The trouble is that my brain has no partitions. It's like a one-room apartment. And if there's another person in there, doing something else while I'm trying to work, I get distracted. I know translators who say that the work goes faster if they do it to music, but their brains must have two, or three, or maybe even eight separate rooms plus an annex with a pool and garage. I really envy them.

JAY RUBIN
on the music of translating

Translating and writing about Haruki Murakami, I could hardly avoid his fixation on music in the development of his style, to the point that "the music of words" made its way into the title of my book about him. It never crossed my mind, though, that music had anything to do with my translation work. If anything, music was as much of an annoyance to me as any other external sound: I have always needed a quiet room for writing. Undeniably, Stan Getz's tenor solo was playing in my head while I translated "The 1963/1982 Girl from Ipanema," but actually turning on the stereo would have ruined my concentration. Haruki's insistence on rhythm in his writing was a point of deep interest, but deliberately imposing some kind of rhythm on an English version of his written words seemed like a stretch. And then it hit me: time after time, I would notice that, halfway through writing an English sentence intended to convey the meaning of an author's Japanese sentence, the rest of the English would come to me not as words but as some kind of preverbal "Bibbidi bobbidi boo"— not definable sounds, but a silent sense of where the emphases would fall and how long the rest of the sentence would be. Only then would the English words come to mind, and, strangely, they would fit into the space that had been formed for them in my brain. I suppose this happened because the words were already there, as suggested by the Japanese but not yet having risen to consciousness in that brief interval. This non-rational, soundlessly musical part of the translation process is what keeps me interested. My goal is someday to end a translated sentence with the strains of "Supercalifragilisticexpialidocious."

ASA YONEDA
on tour

I've always been a little suspicious of recorded music. It has the power to derail you, to sweep you off your feet and whisk you away to unseen worlds, often against your will. It drops you into impossible rooms shaped by spectral plugins, sidetracks you with sweet words tuned to sinister formants, and time-warps you to moments of innocence and revelation you no longer accurately recall—or maybe never actually experienced.

Reading feels safer. Not in the way it tempts you to fill in the gaps with your own false yet revealing backdrops, or the way it can take you into a sharp turn whenever the author chooses. But in the way it lets you shift its key and lean into its tempo depending on which way you want to go. The way it puts you in the driver's seat, bringing the music notated on the page to life in your mind's ear, borrowing the chops of anyone from Kobo Abe to Patti Smith, from Gil Scott-Heron to Kou Machida.

Now imagine taking this sound on the road. You hesitate—you always thought you'd be a writer, not a musician—but you have all the backup you could wish for.

Like the engine and caboose combo of your rhythm section, which hauls you into the pocket and lets you ride the track while you keep your eyes on the stars overhead; or the electric shiver when your voice locks in to the voices of the singers around you, plugging you in to a tractor beam set to a wavelength that illuminates what you want and brings it closer.

Now the only unknown is the crowd. How will they respond to you, the touring member standing in for a recording artist? Do they even notice? Or are they simply happy to be there, let themselves be moved by the music, and enjoy the ride?

HITOMI YOSHIO
on playing from a score

Translating a text from one language to another is akin to
using an instrument to reproduce in sound what is written
on a musical score. When translating from Japanese into
English, sometimes the instrument lacks the ability to
produce the sound notated on the original score. This forces
the translator to be creative with the instrument at hand,
and to craft something that produces a similar effect—or an
entirely different effect but one that is stylistically interesting
or emotionally resonant.

   When the words convey both meaning and rhythm, the
translator must feel the rhythm and work to reproduce the
music behind the words. This is what I did for my translation
of a story by Ichiyō Higuchi that appears in this volume.
Ichiyō's language is concise but deeply intertextual and full
of poetic cadence and allusions. The words expand in the
reader's mind, creating depth in the interpretation and
appreciation of the story. For example, here is a passage from
"The Music of the Koto," where the prose suddenly glides
into the 5-7-5 poetic rhythm:

Chiri no ukiyo no	Scattering from the world
Midare mo nanzo	the dust of worries and troubles,
Matsukaze kayou	like the pine breeze that weaves through
Itono ue niwa	the branches of a willow tree,
Yamahime kitarite	the mountain goddess descends
Te ya souran	and guides her hand over the strings.
Yume mo utsutsu mo	Dream or reality,
Kono uchi ni	the music is ushered in.

   This ethereal description not only gives a sense of how
beautifully the young woman plays her koto but also conveys
the rhythm of the music itself. Sometimes it is necessary to
abandon the poetic rhythm and meter in order to focus more
on words and imagery in the English language that might
capture the essence of what is being conveyed. Translation
is inherently a creative endeavor, but translating poetic
rhythm—the music of the text—requires even more creativity
from the translator. And that's precisely the challenge I look
for when considering what to translate next.

Contributors

JEFFREY ANGLES (b. 1971) is a professor of Japanese language and literature at Western Michigan University. His translation of Hiromi Itō's novel *The Thorn Puller* was published under the Monkey imprint with Stone Bridge Press in 2022. He has also translated eleven other books, including two poetry collections by Hiromi Itō: *Killing Kanoko* and *Wild Grass on the Riverbank* (Tilted Axis, 2020). Angles is also a poet; his book of Japanese-language poems *Watashi no hizukehenkōsen* (My International Date Line) won the 68th Yomiuri Prize for Literature. His essay "Finding Mother" appears in vol. 1 of *MONKEY,* and excerpts from *The Thorn Puller* appear in vols. 1 and 2. His translations of poems by Mutsuo Takahashi are featured in vol. 3 of *MONKEY,* and his translations of microfiction by Taruho Inagaki and Haruki Murakami's "The Zombie" appear in vol. 4.

POLLY BARTON (b. 1984) is a translator of Japanese literature and nonfiction, based in the UK. Recent translations include *Spring Garden* by Tomoka Shibasaki (Pushkin Press, 2017), *Where the Wild Ladies Are* by Aoko Matsuda (Tilted Axis / Soft Skull Press, 2020), *There's No Such Thing as an Easy Job* by Kikuko Tsumura (Bloomsbury, 2021), and *So We Look to the Sky* by Misumi Kubo (Arcade, 2021). After being awarded the 2019 Fitzcarraldo Editions Essay Prize, in 2021 she published *Fifty Sounds,* her reflections on the Japanese language. Her translations of stories by Aoko Matsuda and Tomoka Shibasaki appear in vols. 1–4 of *MONKEY,* and her translations of stories by Kikuko Tsumura appear in vols. 2 and 3.

DAVID BOYD (b. 1981) is an assistant professor of Japanese at the University of North Carolina at Charlotte. He has translated three novellas by Hiroko Oyamada: *The Factory* (2019), *The Hole* (2020), and *Weasels in the Attic* (2022). He won the 2022 Japan-U.S. Friendship Commission Prize for his translation of *The Hole*. With Sam Bett, he has co-translated three novels by Mieko Kawakami: *Breasts and Eggs* (2020), *Heaven* (2021), and *All the Lovers in the Night* (2022). *Heaven* was shortlisted for the International Booker Prize in 2022. His translations of Kuniko Mukōda's "Nori and Eggs for Breakfast" and Kanoko

Okamoto's "Sushi" appear in vol. 1 of *MONKEY*. For vol. 2, he contributed an excerpt from the novel *Takaoka's Travels* by Tatsuhiko Shibusawa. His translations of Hiroko Oyamada's stories appear in vols. 1–4. For vols. 3–4, he co-translated stories by Midori Osaki with Asa Yoneda.

KEVIN BROCKMEIER (b. 1972) is the author of nine books, including the story collections *The Ghost Variations* and *The View from the Seventh Layer* and the novels *The Illumination* and *The Brief History of the Dead*. In 2014 he published *A Few Seconds of Radiant Filmstrip: A Memoir of Seventh Grade*. "Continental Drift" in vol. 7 of *Monkey Business* was inspired by one of Mina Ishikawa's tanka poems, published in vol. 2 of *Monkey Business*. "Time as a Perpetual Motion Machine" appears in vol. 4 of *MONKEY*.

ANDREW CAMPANA (b. 1989) is an assistant professor of Japanese literature at Cornell University. He has been published widely as a translator and as a poet in both English and Japanese. *Expanding Verse: Japanese Poetry at Media's Edge* (University of California Press, 2024) explores how poets have engaged with new technologies such as cinema, tape recording, the internet, and augmented reality. His collection "Seven Modern Poets on Food" was published in vol. 1 of *MONKEY*, "Five Modern Poets on Travel" in vol. 2, "Four Modern Poets on Encounters with Nature" in vol. 3, and "Eight Modern Haiku Poets on Music" in vol. 4.

CHRIS CORKER (b. 1985) is a British-Canadian writer and translator of Japanese fiction and nonfiction. He is currently pursuing doctoral research on the relationship between nostalgia and natural disaster in Japanese literature and film at York University. His translation of an essay by Kengo Kuma is included in *Touch Wood: Material, Architecture, Future,* edited by Carla Ferrer et al. (Zurich: Lars Müller, 2022). His translation of poetry by Keijirō Suga appears in vol. 3 of *MONKEY,* and his translations of poems by Toshiko Hirata, Mizuki Misumi, and Shii appear in vol. 4.

STUART DYBEK (b. 1942) is one of the most important short story writers in the United States today and is also much loved and respected in Japan. His poem "Nowhere" appears in vol. 2 of *Monkey Business,* the short story "Naked" in vol. 4, and "The Crullers" in vol. 5. "Lessons," a poem and a story, appears in vol. 3 of *MONKEY,* and "Swifts, Swallows" in vol. 4.

ANNA ELLIOTT (b. 1963) is the director of the MFA in Literary Translation at Boston University. She is a translator of modern Japanese literature into Polish. Best known for her translations of Haruki Murakami, she has also translated Yukio Mishima, Banana Yoshimoto, and Junichirō Tanizaki. She is the author of a Polish-language monograph on gender in Murakami's writing, a literary guidebook to Murakami's Tokyo, and several articles on Murakami and European translation practices relating to contemporary Japanese fiction.

MICHAEL EMMERICH (b. 1975) teaches Japanese literature at the University of California, Los Angeles. An award-winning translator, he has rendered into English books by Gen'ichirō Takahashi, Hiromi Kawakami, and Hideo Furukawa, among others. He is the author of *The Tale of Genji: Translation, Canonization, and World Literature* (2013) and *Tentekomai: bungaku wa hi kurete michi tōshi* (2018); the editor of *Read Real Japanese Fiction* (2008) and *Short Stories in Japanese: New Penguin Parallel Text* (2011); and the co-editor of *BeHere 1942: A New Lens on the Japanese American Incarceration* (2022). His translations of Masatsugu Ono, Makoto Takayanagi, and others are featured in *Monkey Business* and *MONKEY*.

KAORI FUJINO (b. 1980) is an award-winning author. Her debut work of fiction, "Greedy Birds," was awarded the Bungakukai Newcomers Prize in 2006, and her novel *Nails and Eyes* won the Akutagawa Prize in 2013. In 2017 she was a resident at the University of Iowa's International Writing Program. Her story "You Okay for Time?" was translated by Ginny Tapley Takemori and appeared in *Granta* in 2017. "Someday with the One, the Perfect Bag," translated by Laurel Taylor, is featured in vol. 3 of *MONKEY* and "Transformers: Pianos" in vol. 4.

HIDEO FURUKAWA (b. 1966) is one of the most innovative writers in Japan today. His novel *Belka, Why Don't You Bark?* was translated by Michael Emmerich; his partly fictional reportage *Horses, Horses, in the End the Light Remains Pure: A Tale That Begins with Fukushima* was translated by Doug Slaymaker with Akiko Takenaka; and his short novel *Slow Boat* was translated by David Boyd. His work appears in every issue of *Monkey Business* and *MONKEY*; vol. 1 of *Monkey Business* features an interview with Haruki Murakami by Hideo Furukawa; vol. 3 of *MONKEY* features "The Little Woods of Fukushima," an excerpt from his memoir *Zero F*; vol. 4 includes an excerpt from his epic poem *Ten-On*.

TED GOOSSEN (b. 1948) is a literary translator and one of the founding editors of *Monkey Business* and *MONKEY New Writing from Japan.* He is the editor of *The Oxford Book of Japanese Short Stories.* He translated Haruki Murakami's *Wind/Pinball* and *The Strange Library,* and co-translated (with Philip Gabriel) *Men Without Women* and *Killing Commendatore.* His translations of Hiromi Kawakami's *People from My Neighborhood* and Naoya Shiga's *Reconciliation* were published in 2020. His translation of *Dragon Palace* by Hiromi Kawakami was published under the MONKEY imprint with Stone Bridge Press in 2023. His translations of Murakami, Shiga, Kawakami, and others are featured in every issue of *Monkey Business* and in *MONKEY,* vols. 1–4.

MIMI HACHIKAI (b. 1974) is an award-winning poet and novelist and a professor at Rikkyo University. Her collections of poetry include the 2015 *Water for Washing Your Face,* winner of the Ayukawa Nobuo Prize. She has translated several children's books, including *The Dark* by Lemony Snicket. "Just Like Her" was first published in vol. 28 of the Japanese *MONKEY.*

KENDALL HEITZMAN (b. 1973) is an associate professor of Japanese literature and culture at the University of Iowa. He has translated stories and essays by Kaori Fujino, Nori Nakagami, Tomoka Shibasaki, and Yūshō Takiguchi. He is the author of *Enduring Postwar: Yasuoka Shōtarō and Literary Memory in Japan* (Vanderbilt University Press, 2019). His translation of Kaori Fujino's *Nails and Eyes* was published by Pushkin Press in 2023. His translations of the work of Hideo Furukawa appear in *MONKEY,* vols. 3–4.

ICHIYŌ HIGUCHI (1872–1896) was a celebrated poet and short story writer. She studied classical poetry at Haginoya under Utako Nakajima. Following her father's death, she became head of the household at the age of seventeen and began to write stories to help support her mother and sister. She also ran a small shop near the Yoshiwara pleasure quarters, which became the setting for many of her later stories. A selection of Ichiyō's writings was published in translation by Robert Lyons Danly in his critical biography *In the Shade of Spring Leaves.* "The Music of the Koto," translated by Hitomi Yoshio, appears in vol. 4 of *MONKEY.*

TOSHIKO HIRATA (b. 1955) is a poet and novelist known for witty wordplay and wickedly dark humor. Her 2015 collection of poetry *Freedom of Quips* won the Murasaki Shikibu Literary Award. "Rain Clouds" was first published in vol. 28 of the Japanese *MONKEY.*

LISA HOFMANN-KURODA (b. 1987) is a literary translator. Born in Tokyo, raised in Texas, she received her BA from Wesleyan University and her PhD from UC Berkeley. She is an active member of the ALTA BIPOC Translators' Caucus and a two-time graduate of the British Centre for Literary Translation. With Allison Markin Powell, she is the translator of Ryūnosuke Akutagawa's *Kappa* (New Directions, 2023). Her translations of Shun Medoruma, Sachiko Kishimoto, and Yōko Uema appear in *The Baffler, Chicago Review,* and *Guernica.* Her translations of Natsuo Kirino's *The Swallow Does Not Return* (Knopf) and Yōko Tawada's *Exophony* (New Directions) will be published in 2024.

IKO IDOGAWA (b. 1987) is a poet and novelist and teaches Japanese at a high school. She was the winner of the prestigious Akutagawa Prize in 2022 with her second novel *The Joy of This World*. "Someday, my annihilation will come" was first published in vol. 28 of the Japanese *MONKEY*.

TARUHO INAGAKI (1900–1977) was a prolific Japanese modernist writer known for his highly idiosyncratic voice and vision, which by the 1970s had gathered a cult-like following in Japan. While a young student at an international school in Kobe, he became fascinated with other cultures, aeronautics, astronomy, and attractive young men—interests that recur throughout his oeuvre. His books include the playful collection *One Thousand One-Second Stories* (1923), from which Jeffrey Angles has translated 11 pieces for this issue, *Miroku* (1946), and the award-winning essay collection *The Aesthetics of Boy-Love* (1968).

SEIKŌ ITŌ (b. 1961) is a writer, performer, and one of the pioneers of Japanese rap. His novel *Imagination Radio* (2013) reflects on the March 2011 earthquake and nuclear disaster through the eyes of a deejay. He also writes nonfiction, including a 2017 book on Doctors Without Borders. Itō has long been interested in Noh, and he and Jay Rubin have collaborated with Grand Master Kazufusa Hōshō in a contemporary performance of the traditional Noh play *Hagoromo*. Rubin's translation of Itō's *Fujito* appears in vol. 1 of *MONKEY*, *Kurozuka* in vol. 2, *Tadanori* in vol. 3, and *Takasago* in vol. 4.

HIROMI KAWAKAMI (b. 1958) is one of Japan's leading novelists. Many of her books have been published in English, most recently the story collection *Dragon Palace* and the novel *The Third Love*, both translated by Ted Goossen. Other titles include *Manazuru*, translated by Michael Emmerich; *Record of a Night Too Brief*, translated by Lucy North; and *The Nakano Thrift Shop, Parade: A Folktale, Strange Weather in Tokyo* (shortlisted for the Man Asian Literary Prize in 2013), and *The Ten Loves of Nishino*, translated by Allison Markin Powell. "The Dragon Palace" appears in vol. 3 of *Monkey Business*, and "Hazuki and Me"

in vol. 5. "Banana," which was published in vol. 4 of *Monkey Business*, is included in *The Best Small Fictions 2015* (Queen's Ferry Press). "Sea Horse" appears in vol. 2 of *MONKEY*, and an excerpt from *The Third Love* in vol. 4. *People from My Neighborhood*, translated by Ted Goossen, was published by Granta Books in 2020 and Soft Skull Press in 2021. The series continues to be featured in both the Japanese and English editions of *MONKEY*.

MIEKO KAWAKAMI (b. 1976) is an award-winning novelist and poet. Her novel *Breasts and Eggs*, translated by Sam Bett and David Boyd, was published by Europa Editions in 2020 to great acclaim. *Heaven*, also co-translated by Bett and Boyd, was published in 2021, and *All the Lovers in the Night* in 2022. Her short novel *Ms Ice Sandwich* (Pushkin Press, 2018) was translated by Louise Heal Kawai. Her stories and prose poems, translated by Hitomi Yoshio, appear in vols. 1–7 of *Monkey Business*. "Good Stories Originate in the Caves of Antiquity," a conversation with Haruki Murakami, was published in *MONKEY*, vol. 1; "Seeing," a poem, appears in *MONKEY*, vol. 2; "Upon Seeing the Evening Sky," an essay, in vol. 3; and "The Day Before," a poem, in vol. 4.

SACHIKO KISHIMOTO (b. 1960) is known for her translations of Nicholson Baker, Lucia Berlin, Judy Budnitz, Lydia Davis, Thom Jones, and Miranda July. She is also a popular essayist; her latest collection, *Seas I'd Like to See Before I Die*, appeared in 2020. Excerpts from *The Forbidden Diary*, a fictional diary, translated by Ted Goossen, are featured in vols. 1–7 of *Monkey Business*. "Misaki" appears in vol. 1 of *MONKEY*, and "I Don't Remember" in vol. 3.

SATOSHI KITAMURA (b. 1956) is an award-winning picture-book author and illustrator. His own books include *Stone Age Boy, Millie's Marvellous Hat*, and *The Smile Shop*. He has worked with numerous authors and poets. His graphic narratives are featured in vols. 5–7 of *Monkey Business*: "Mr. Quote" in vol. 7, "Igor Nocturnov" in vol. 6, and "Variation and Theme," inspired by a Charles Simic poem, in vol. 5. In vol. 1 of *MONKEY*, he published "The Heart of the Lunchbox";

"The Overcoat" appears in vol. 2, "The Cave" in vol. 3, and "Five Parallel Lines" in vol. 4, to which he also contributed the cover illustration.

SAM MALISSA (b. 1981) holds a PhD in Japanese literature from Yale University. His translations include *Bullet Train* by Kōtaro Isaka (Harvill Secker, 2021), *The End of the Moment We Had* by Toshiki Okada (Pushkin Press, 2018), and short fiction by Shun Medoruma, Hideo Furukawa, and Masatsugu Ono. His translations of stories by Kyōhei Sakaguchi appear in vols. 1–4 of *MONKEY.*

AOKO MATSUDA (b. 1979) is a writer and translator. In 2013 her debut *Stackable* was nominated for the Mishima Yukio Prize and the Noma Literary New Face Prize. In 2019 her short story "The Woman Dies" (from the collection *The Year of No Wild Flowers*), translated by Polly Barton and published by Granta online, was shortlisted for a Shirley Jackson Award. And in 2021, *Where the Wild Ladies Are,* translated by Polly Barton, won a World Fantasy Award in the best collection category. Her short novel *The Girl Who Is Getting Married* was published by Strangers Press in 2016. She has translated work by Karen Russell, Amelia Gray, and Carmen Maria Machado into Japanese. Her stories appear in vols. 5–7 of *Monkey Business,* translated by Jeffrey Angles. "Dissecting Misogyny," "The Most Boring Red on Earth," "A Father and His Back," and "Angels and Electricity," translated by Polly Barton, appear in vols. 1–4 of *MONKEY.*

MIZUKI MISUMI (b. 1981) has published nine volumes of poetry, including *Overkill,* the 2005 Nakahara Chūya Prize winner, and *A Room Without Neighbors,* the 2014 Hagiwara Sakutarō Prize winner. "Reach Out Those Young Limbs" was first published in vol. 28 of the Japanese *MONKEY.*

MARGARET MITSUTANI (b. 1953) is a translator living in Tokyo. Her translations of short stories by Kyoko Hayashi have appeared in *Manoa* and *Prairie Schooner.* She has also translated works by Kenzaburo Oe, Mitsuyo Kakuta, and Yoko Tawada. Her translation of Tawada's *The Emissary* (New Directions, 2018)

won both the National Book Award for Translated Literature and the Miyoshi Award. Tawada's *Scattered All Over the Earth* (New Directions, 2022), the first volume of a trilogy, was short-listed for the National Book Award for Translated Literature. *Suggested in the Stars,* volume two of the trilogy, is forthcoming from New Directions.

HARUKI MURAKAMI (b. 1949) is one of the world's best-known and best-loved novelists. All his major novels—including *Hardboiled Wonderland and the End of the World, The Wind-Up Bird Chronicle,* and *1Q84*—have been translated into dozens of languages. "On Writing Short Stories" in vol. 7 of *Monkey Business* is the second half of his conversation with Motoyuki Shibata, published in vol. 9 (Summer/Fall 2016) of the Japanese *MONKEY.* An interview by Hideo Furukawa appears in vol. 1 of *Monkey Business.* His essays "The Great Cycle of Storytelling" and "So What Shall I Write About?" appear in vol. 2 and vol. 5 of *Monkey Business.* Vol. 4 of *Monkey Business* includes an essay by Richard Powers on Murakami's fiction. "Good Stories Originate in the Caves of Antiquity," a conversation with Mieko Kawakami, appears in vol. 1 of *MONKEY,* the essay "Jogging in Southern Europe" in vol. 2, the story "Creta Kano," translated by Gitte Hansen, in vol. 3, and "The Zombie," translated by Jeffrey Angles, in vol. 4.

SAWAKO NAKAYASU (b. 1975) is an artist working with language, performance, and translation— separately and in various combinations. Her most recent books include *Pink Waves* (Omnidawn), a finalist for the PEN/Voelcker award; *Some Girls Walk into the Country They Are From* (Wave Books); and the pamphlet *Say Translation Is Art* (Ugly Duckling Presse). Translations include *The Collected Poems of Chika Sagawa* (Modern Library) and *Mouth: Eats Color—Sagawa Chika Translations, Anti-translations, & Originals* (Rogue Factorial), a multilingual work of both original and translated poetry.

SAYAKA ŌSAKI (b. 1982) is a poet, and her second collection of poetry, *Pointing Impossible,* was awarded the 2014 Nakahara Chūya Prize. She has also written

two children's books. "I Cook, and Eat" was first published in vol. 28 of the Japanese *MONKEY.*

MIDORI OSAKI (1896–1971) was a modernist writer.
Born in Tottori prefecture, she was most active in the
1920s and 1930s. Her best-known work, "Wandering
in the Realm of the Seventh Sense," was translated
by Kyoko Selden and Alisa Freedman. "Walking,"
translated by Asa Yoneda and David Boyd, appears in
vol. 3 of *MONKEY,* and "Cricket Girl" appears in vol. 4.
Hitomi Yoshio's translation of the 1929 play "Apple
Pie Afternoon" is featured on the MONKEY website
under "Translators to watch for." Her life was the
subject of the 1998 film *Wandering in the Realm of the
Seventh Sense: In Search of Midori Osaki* by pink film
director Sachi Hamano.

HIROKO OYAMADA (b. 1983) is one of Japan's most
promising young writers. Her short novels *The Factory,
The Hole,* and *Weasels in the Attic* were translated
by David Boyd and published by New Directions. Her
story "Spider Lily" was translated by Juliet Winters
Carpenter and published in the Japan issue of
Granta (Spring 2014). "Lost in the Zoo" and "Extra
Innings," translated by David Boyd, appear in vols. 6
and 7 of *Monkey Business.* "Something Sweet," "Along
the Embankment," "Turtles," and "Flight," also
translated by David Boyd, are featured in *MONKEY,*
vols. 1–4.

JAY RUBIN (b. 1941) is professor emeritus of Japanese
literature at Harvard University. One of the principal
translators of Haruki Murakami, he translated
*The Wind-Up Bird Chronicle, Norwegian Wood,
After Dark, 1Q84* (co-translated with Philip Gabriel),
After the Quake: Stories, and *Absolutely on Music:
Conversations with Seiji Ozawa.* Among his many
other translations are *Rashōmon and Seventeen Other
Stories* by Ryūnosuke Akutagawa and *The Miner*
and *Sanshirō* by Sōseki Natsume. He is the author of
Haruki Murakami and the Music of Words and the
editor of *The Penguin Book of Japanese Short Stories.*
His translations into English of Seikō Itō's modern
Japanese translations of Noh plays appear in every
issue of *MONKEY.*

KYŌHEI SAKAGUCHI (b. 1978) is a writer, artist,
and architect. His work explores alternative ways of
being, as in his books *Zero Yen House* and *Build Your
Own Independent Nation.* His novel *Haikai Taxi*
was nominated for the Yukio Mishima Prize in 2014.
Translated by Sam Malissa, "Forest of the Ronpa"
appears in vol. 1 of *MONKEY,* "The Lake" in vol. 2,
"The Tale of Malig the Navigator" in vol. 3, and "Listen
for the Perfume" in vol. 4.

TOMOKA SHIBASAKI (b. 1973) is a novelist, short
story writer, and essayist. Her books include *Awake or
Asleep, Viridian,* and *In the City Where I Wasn't.* She
won the Akutagawa Prize in 2014 with *Spring Garden,*
which has been translated by Polly Barton (Pushkin
Press). "The Seaside Road" appears in vol. 2 of *Monkey
Business,* "The Glasses Thief" in vol. 3, "Background
Music" in vol. 6, translated by Ted Goossen, and
"Peter and Janis" in vol. 7, translated by Christopher
Lowy. Her stories, translated by Polly Barton, are
featured in vols. 1–4 of *MONKEY.*

MOTOYUKI SHIBATA (b. 1954) translates American
literature and runs the Japanese literary journal
MONKEY. He has translated Paul Auster, Rebecca
Brown, Stuart Dybek, Steve Erickson, Brian Evenson,
Laird Hunt, Kelly Link, Steven Millhauser, and
Richard Powers, among others. His translation
of Mark Twain's *Adventures of Huckleberry Finn* was
a bestseller in Japan in 2018. His recent translations
include Eric McCormack's *Cloud* and Jonathan Swift's
Gulliver's Travels. He is professor emeritus at the
University of Tokyo.

SHII is the pen name of a poet who often combines
poetry with her own photography. She was the
2020 winner of the Contemporary Poetry Notebook
Award. "For Yoko Sensei" was first published in
vol. 28 of the Japanese *MONKEY.*

MAKOTO TAKAYANAGI (b. 1950) has published
numerous books of poetry. His collected works
appeared in two volumes in 2016. A third volume was
published in 2019. *Aliceland* was his first publication,
in 1980; a translation by Michael Emmerich appears in

vol. 7 of *Monkey Business*. "Five Prose Poems" appears in vol. 1 of *MONKEY,* "The Graffiti" in vol. 3, and selections from *For the Transcription of Interstellar Music* in vol. 4 (all translated by Michael Emmerich).

LAUREL TAYLOR (b. 1989) is a translator, writer, and PhD student in Japanese and comparative literature at Washington University in St. Louis. She holds an MFA in literary translation from the University of Iowa and currently works as an assistant managing editor for *Asymptote.* Her translations include fiction and poetry by Yaeko Batchelor, Aoko Matsuda, Noriko Mizuta, and Tomoka Shibasaki. Her translations of stories by Kaori Fujino appear in vols. 3–4 of *MONKEY.*

ASA YONEDA (b. 198Q) is the translator of *The Lonesome Bodybuilder* (Soft Skull Press, 2018) by Yukiko Motoya and *Idol, Burning* (HarperVia/ Canongate, 2022) by Rin Usami. With David Boyd, Yoneda is co-editing *KANATA,* a collection of Japanese fiction chapbooks for Strangers Press. "Walking" by Midori Osaki, co-translated with David Boyd, appears in vol. 3 of *MONKEY,* and Osaki's "Cricket Girl" appears in vol. 4. Yoneda's translation of "The City Bird" by Natsuko Kuroda is also featured in vol. 3.

HITOMI YOSHIO (b. 1979) is associate professor of Global Japanese Literary and Cultural Studies at Waseda University. Her main area of research is modern and contemporary Japanese literature with a focus on women's writing and literary communities. During 2022–24 she has been a visiting scholar at Harvard University. Her translation of Midori Osaki's play "Apple Pie Afternoon" is featured on the MONKEY website under "Translators to watch for." She is the translator of Natsuko Imamura's *This Is Amiko, Do You Copy?* (Pushkin Press, 2023) and is the co-translator of Mieko Kawakami's two forthcoming short story collections. Her translations of Mieko Kawakami's work are featured in every issue of *MONKEY*; vol. 4 includes her translation of "The Music of the Koto" by Ichiyō Higuchi.

ROB WINGER (b. 1974) is the author of four books of poetry, most recently *It Doesn't Matter What We*

Meant (Penguin Random House Canada, 2021). He's been shortlisted for a Governor General's Literary Award, the Trillium Book Award for Poetry, and the Ottawa Book Award. He lives in the hills northeast of Toronto, where he teaches English and creative writing at Trent University.

Credits

Permissions have been secured with the authors. The translators hold copyright to their translations.

Page 5: Illustration © Satoshi Kitamura.

Pages 6–7: *Tsukasa and Other Courtesans of the Ōgiya Watching the Autumn Moon Rise Over the Rice Fields from a Balcony in the Yoshiwara,* Katsushika Hokusai, woodblock print, 1799; courtesy of the Cleveland Museum of Art.

Page 17: Artwork © Kenji Kobayashi.

Page 23: Illustration © Toko Hosoya.

Page 39: *Impact,* mixed media on paper, 2023 © Manny Trinh.

Pages 46–47: Illustration © Satoshi Kitamura.

Pages 48: Illustration © Sara Wong / TOOGL.

Pages 55: *Ten-On,* collage (drawing by Keisuke Kondo, photograph by Hideo Furukawa), 2022 © Keisuke Kondo.

Page 60: Illustration © Sam Messer.

Page 68: Original album cover designed by Michel Otthoffer for *Le Koto de Hiromu Handa,* 1977. Source: dcphoto / Alamy Stock Photo.

Pages 73–79: Graphic vignettes © Satoshi Kitamura.

Page 80: Photographs taken in Rasht, Iran, by Hamed Rajabpour; design by Nariman Ghorbani. Source: Creative Commons Attribution-Share Alike 4.0 International.

Page 88: *Me When I'm Changing,* pastel on paper, 2023 © Kyōhei Sakaguchi.

Page 92: Photograph © Yoshiaki Kanda.

Page 114: Composition © TOOGL using photos from stock.adobe.com: blue and orange sunset sky by sutichak; flying swallows, photo by Konstiantyn; and gargoyle on Notre Dame Cathedral, photo by sborisov.

Page 119: Illustration © Satoshi Kitamura.

Page 120: Composition © TOOGL using a still of Fiona Macleod, played by Delcea Mihaela Gabriela from the 2006 film *The Cricket Girl,* directed by Sachi Hamano © Tantansha, and paulownia empress tree plant by Charles Dessalines D'orbigny © rawpixel.

Page 128: Illustration © Lauren Tamaki.

Page 137: Illustration © Alina Skyson / TOOGL.

"Each issue is as purposely crafted as a good novel." —*John Irving*

**SUBSCRIBE TODAY AT
BRICKMAG.COM**

@BRICKLITERARY

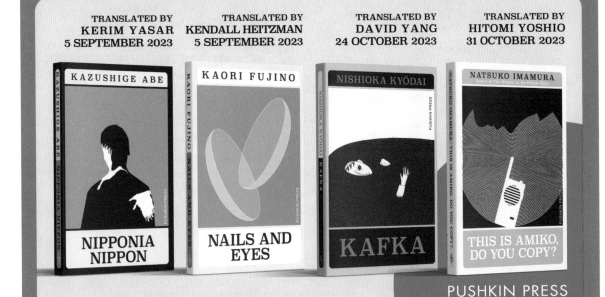

TRANSLATED BY	TRANSLATED BY	TRANSLATED BY	TRANSLATED BY
KERIM YASAR	**KENDALL HEITZMAN**	**DAVID YANG**	**HITOMI YOSHIO**
5 SEPTEMBER 2023	**5 SEPTEMBER 2023**	**24 OCTOBER 2023**	**31 OCTOBER 2023**

KAZUSHIGE ABE
NIPPONIA NIPPON

KAORI FUJINO
NAILS AND EYES

NISHIOKA KYŌDAI
KAFKA

NATSUKO IMAMURA
THIS IS AMIKO, DO YOU COPY?

PUSHKIN PRESS

SHORT, CUTTING-EDGE WORKS FROM OUTSTANDING VOICES IN JAPANESE FICTION

'Awesome' Patti Smith   'Excellent' Claudia Winkleman

WEASELS IN THE ATTIC

HIROKO OYAMADA

Out now in paperback from the award-winning Japanese novelist

'Deeply unsettling... The book simmers with eerie tension and bursts with unforgettable monologues' NPR

GRANTA

See where MONKEY began

monkey business
new writing from japan

Featuring the best in Japanese contemporary fiction today, including:

- Mieko Kawakami
- Yōko Ogawa
- Haruki Murakami
- Aoko Matsuda
- Hiromi Kawakami
- Hideo Furukawa
- Hiromi Itō
- Makoto Takayanagi
- Tomoka Shibasaki
- Sachiko Kishimoto
- Hiroko Oyamada

and many more!

All seven volumes available as ebooks
Volumes 5, 6, and 7 are still available in print, while supplies last!

 Purchase today at
monkeybusinessmag.com/shop

MONKEY

CONTEMPORARY JAPANESE FICTION IN TRANSLATION

The MONKEY imprint at Stone Bridge Press is proud to announce the publication of **DRAGON PALACE** by Hiromi Kawakami, translated by Ted Goossen.

" Kawakami has a remarkable ability to obscure reality, fantasy, and memory, making the desire for love feel hauntingly real.
—**PUBLISHERS WEEKLY**

" How can a person resist?
—**PARIS REVIEW**

" In these stories, troubled lives are forever changed by supernatural forces.
—**EILEEN GONZALEZ,** *FOREWORD*

From the bestselling author of *Strange Weather in Tokyo* comes this otherworldly collection of eight stories, each a masterpiece of transformation, infused with humor, sex, and the universal search for love and beauty—in a world where the laws of time and space, and even species boundaries, don't apply. Meet a shape-shifting con man, a goddess who uses sex to control her followers, an elderly man possessed by a fox spirit, a woman who falls in love with her 400-year-old ancestor, a kitchen god with three faces in an apartment block infested by weasels, moles who provide sanctuary underground for humans who have lost the will to live, a man nurtured through life by his seven extraordinary sisters, and a woman who is handed from husband to husband until she is finally able to return to the sea.

PRINT 978-1-7376253-5-3   EBOOK 978-1-7376253-6-0

Distributed to bookstores worldwide and online by Consortium
sbp@stonebridge.com   www.stonebridge.com

MONKEY

CONTEMPORARY JAPANESE FICTION IN TRANSLATION

> ❝ A lyrical account of a woman caught between two cultures and her family's demands.
>
> —**PUBLISHERS WEEKLY**

> ❝ Embellished with all manner of welcoming, unfiltered, surprisingly humorous honesty about the universally quotidian, from pimple-popping to good sex.
>
> —**TERRY HONG,** *BOOKLIST*

> ❝ One of the best Japanese novels in translation in recent years.
>
> —**ERIC MARGOLIS,** *JAPAN TIMES*

> ❝ How wonderful to find the rhythm of the Japanese reproduced so marvelously in this translation!
>
> —**YOKO TAWADA, AUTHOR OF** *THE EMISSARY*

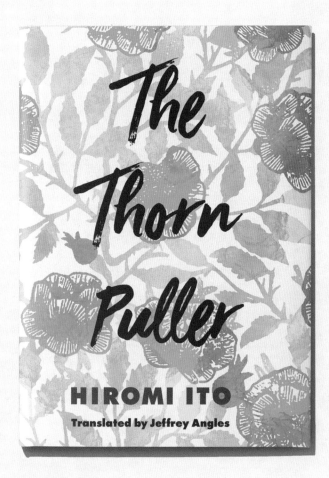

Just some of the wide acclaim for **THE THORN PULLER,** a novel by Hiromi Ito, translated by Jeffrey Angles and published by the MONKEY imprint at Stone Bridge Press.

PRINT 978-1-7376253-0-8   EBOOK 978-1-7376253-1-5

Distributed to bookstores worldwide and online by Consortium
sbp@stonebridge.com   www.stonebridge.com

FOOD   TRAVEL   CROSSINGS

GRAB YOUR OWN COPY TODAY

Volume 1: FOOD and volume 2: TRAVEL helped us through the pandemic.

In volume 3: CROSSINGS, we emerged, inspired by stories of transformation and the joyful play between Japanese and Western literatures.

"

MONKEY is an event to be celebrated.
—**LINDSAY SEMEL,** *ASYMPTOTE*

"

Wild, dizzying fun.
—**ERIC MARGOLIS,** *JAPAN TIMES*

"

Literary, curated by the best, and vibrating in the curious space between English and Japanese.
—**CRAIG MOD,** *RIDGELINE*

Print books are also distributed to bookstores worldwide and online by Consortium
sbp@stonebridge.com   www.stonebridge.com

Available in full-color print and ebook.

Purchase today at
monkeymagazine.org/shop

**MONKEY CELEBRATES
MONKEY New Writing from Japan**

SWITCH PUBLISHING   www.switch-store.net